THE LAST

BOYFRIEND

Forever Love – Book One

J.S. COOPER

THE LAST

BOYFRIEND

PROLOGUE

HE WASN'T SURE WHY HE ALWAYS chose this diner. It was a risky thing to do. If any of the waitresses slipped up and mentioned something about all of his dates here, it could ruin everything. All he knew was that he liked this diner: it was low-key, comfortable, and relaxing. It allowed him to entertain the girls without feeling any pressure. They were all beautiful women, and he was able to get what he wanted from them easily. They were everything he wanted and nothing he needed. If he was honest with himself, he knew that he liked it that way. He wasn't going to allow a woman to get under his skin. He was never going to change his mind about falling in love. Not for anyone, and certainly not for a brunette named Lucky, whom he barely knew. He had to be focused on the plan at hand, and he couldn't allow emotions to get in the way of what he needed to do.

CHAPTER ONE

"CAN YOU BELIEVE THIS GUY IS in here again with another girl?" Shayla peered out into the dining room and shook her head. "Are these girls stupid?"

"Maybe they don't care?" I shrugged, indifferent to how many different dates Mr. Big Tipper brought to the restaurant every Friday night.

"Or they don't know." She rolled her eyes as she prepared two garden salads for her latest customer.

"But really, how can they not know? One look at him tells you that he's a guy who's not going to be faithful."

"Shayla," I laughed as I sorted through mountains of silverware and wrapped sets of them into napkins. "You can't judge a book by its cover."

"So you would go on a date with him if he asked you?"

"Oh, hell no." I laughed and looked out at the tall, handsome jock sitting at one of my tables. His name was Zane Beaumont, and he had been frequenting Lou's Burger Joint every Friday night for the last three months with a different girl each time. This week's date seemed as vapid as all the other girls he had previously brought into the diner. But I was no longer surprised—not like Shayla was—every time he walked in with a new girl. In fact, I would have been more surprised if he came in with the same girl two weeks in a row.

"You don't think he's hot?" Shayla turned to me and wriggled her eyebrows before heading off to deliver her salads.

"Oh, he's hot all right." I laughed again and stared at him, studying his face clinically. "But he must be the biggest player in Miami." Zane Beaumont was everything I wanted to avoid in a guy. He was too handsome to be a good guy, with his light blue eyes and dark brown, slightly too-long hair. His hair was always perfectly spiked, with a wisp in his face that looked like he'd combed through with his fingers to give it a tousled look. His face was chiseled and classically handsome and always had a slightly smug and superior look on it. There was something about his persona that I was instinctively attracted to. But I knew there was no way I would ever act on the attraction I felt—not that he would ever be interested in me, anyway.

"You should go for it, girl." Maria, the other waitress working that evening, wriggled her eyebrows at me as she finished counting out her tips. "He always sits at your table. I bet he has a crush on you, *chica*."

"Thanks for the vote of confidence, Maria, but I doubt it." I laughed easily while a warm flush ran through my body. "Even if he was interested, which he isn't, I would never date someone like him. There's no way that he would fit my rules."

"Ay, *dios mio.*" Maria rolled her eyes. "You talking about those rules again? Forget the rules. Just go with the flow."

"You know I can't do that, Maria." I sighed. "I created the rules for a reason. I don't want to just be some guy's bed buddy anymore. I'm saving myself for the real deal."

"If you say so." She stuffed a thick wad of cash into her handbag and jumped up. "But I'm sure he would be dynamite in the sack if you were to change your mind." She laughed, and I had to nod in agreement.

There was something in the way Zane Beaumont moved that was rhythmic and sexy. Plus, his hands were large, warm, and manly. I flushed as I remembered the shock of electricity I felt each time our fingers touched when I took his payments.

"Bye, Maria. I'll see you tomorrow?"

"No, *chica*, me and Pedro are going salsa dancing." She grinned and did a couple of steps in the kitchen.

"Oh, that should be fun." I smiled at her, slightly envious. I wish I could afford to take Saturday nights off. Not that it actually mattered anyway. I didn't have a boyfriend, and my two best friends were coupled up. So when I did have the night off, I was usually at home by myself, watching crappy movies, with a large tub of Ben & Jerry's Phish Food ice cream.

"You should come with us one night, girl. Pedro's cousin just moved here from New York, his name's Armando. I think you'd like him."

"That's okay. Thanks, Maria." I laughed and quickly made my way into the dining hall as a new couple was seated at my table.

I sighed as they got into the booth on the same side. They were obviously a new couple, trying to cozy up together as much as possible. It was hard working at the diner on Friday and Saturday nights because they were usually date nights. But they were also the best nights for tips. Zane Beaumont always tipped me at least fifty percent—what girl could say no to that?

"Hi, I'm Lucky, I'll be your server tonight. Can I start you off with any drinks?" I kept the smile plastered on my face, even though the couple paid no attention to me. They were too busy kissing. "Or maybe I'll give you a few minutes." I walked away from the table as they continued to ignore me, and went to check up on Zane and his date.

"Hi, is everything going okay?" I smiled pleasantly, trying to ignore the excitement in my stomach as Zane stared up at me attentively with a sexy smile.

"Is this Diet Coke?" The beautiful brunette asked with an attitude. "I asked for Diet Coke and this tastes like regular Coke."

"I can assure you that this is Diet Coke, ma'am." I tried to make sure I didn't roll my eyes. "I personally filled your drink order, and I made sure to hit the Diet Coke button."

"Well, are you sure? Because it doesn't taste like Diet Coke." She glared at me.

I turned to Zane. "Is there anything else you need, Mr. Beaumont?"

"I told you to call me Zane." He laughed. "And no, we're good here. Thank you, Lucky."

"My pleasure." I smiled and walked back into the kitchen grinning. I would never admit it to Shayla or Maria, but I loved seeing Zane Beaumont every week. In fact, seeing him was the only thing that kept me sane and from dying of loneliness. I had been single for a year now—no dates, no kisses, and certainly no sex, and it was starting to wear on me. I had been asked out by a few guys, but none I would give the time of day to—and certainly none whom I found as attractive as Zane.

Not only were my work friends shocked at my lack of dates, so were Leeza and Shannon, my two best friends. The three of us had bonded during Freshmen Week at the University of Miami and had been regulars at pretty much every party on campus for our first two years. We had all gone from boyfriend to boyfriend, and I thought nothing of our dating habits. That is, until about a year ago, when my boyfriend at the time, a graduating senior who was also the president of his fraternity, Sigma Chi, broke up with me. It had pretty much devastated me, and it was his closing words that had the biggest impact on me: "You didn't think this was serious, right, Lucky? Everyone knows you're the girl for a fun time. How many guys have you been with since you started UM? You're like a hurricane with guys." And then he had laughed at his joke. "Hurricane—get it?" He had asked, and I had nodded wordlessly.

The fact that he had jokingly compared my dating history to the school's football team's mascot was not funny to me. He had made me feel like a slut, like I was one of those girls who just went from guy to guy and bed to bed. I knew he thought that I was that kind of girl, but I really wasn't. At least not in the way he had thought. It was true that I had dated about eight different guys during my three years at UM. But I had only slept with three of them. Apparently, the five I didn't sleep with didn't pass that information on when they talked about me.

It had taken me about a month to get over the hurt and pain, and I had made a decision with myself—that I wasn't going to date just to date anymore. I wanted to make sure that any guy I dated had the possibility of being my last boyfriend. I had a last-boyfriend plan and that meant he had to fit a number of criteria:

1.   He had to be honest.

2.   He had to be good-looking but not too hot or he would have too many women after him, something I knew from experience.

3.   He had to be looking for a serious relationship, but not be too old or too desperate about settling down.

4.   He had to be financially secure but not too rich, or too many women would be after him; once again, something I knew from experience.

5.   He had to be funny, loyal, faithful, and modest.

6.   He had to agree to wait for sex until we were married or engaged.

I figured I had created a pretty thorough list. Shayla, Maria, Shannon, and Leeza all thought I was being ridiculous with my list and was destined for a lifetime of singledom. But I explained to them that I wasn't looking to just date anyone—I was looking for the guy who would be my last boyfriend. This was the only way I could ensure that I didn't get my heart stomped on again.

So now, here I was, a year later at twenty-two and just about to graduate from college with no current boyfriend and none in sight.

Zane Beaumont was the type of guy I would have gone for in a heartbeat before I created the list. But he was also the type of guy that I knew would take my heart and rip it to pieces.

"Hey, Lucky, your new table is ready to order." Shayla came running into the kitchen with a plate in her hands. "And Mike, they asked for white meat, not dark. You need to do the white meat special again, please, and quickly. I don't want to miss out on another tip."

"Gotcha, Shayla." Mike grinned and dropped some chicken into the deep fryer. He winked at her and she sighed before turning to me with an exasperated look on her face. "I tell ya, I don't think it's smart to work with your boyfriend."

"You wouldn't have it any other way, Shay." I grinned at her before going back into the dining room. Shayla and Mike had an almost perfect relationship. They had both been working at Lou's for over five years before Mike decided to ask her out on a date, and they had been together ever since.

"Hi, are you guys ready to order now?"

"We'd like a cheeseburger and fries." The guy ordered for both of them, while the girl just sat there grinning. "We're going to share, so put the pickles on the side, please."

"And the onions, too." The girl finally spoke, and they both laughed.

"Okay, so a cheeseburger and fries? Anything else?"

"No, just two waters." And then they were back to kissing again.

I walked to the fountain to get them two glasses of water and sighed. There wasn't going to be a big tip coming from them, I was sure of that. I tried to calculate how much money I had made for the night and bit my lip. I still hadn't made enough to take my car to a mechanic. My 1991 Toyota Corolla was on its last legs, and I was pretty sure the head gasket was going to blow again. It was exhibiting the same signs about a year ago when it had blown, and I knew I couldn't afford to be without my car now. I wouldn't be able to get to school and work if I didn't have my car, and I sure couldn't afford to buy a new one. But the mechanic wanted eight hundred dollars to fix my car and I only had about five hundred. I had been hoping that tonight I would have some spend-happy, hungry customers from South America, but I hadn't been so lucky. "I guess maybe tomorrow will be my night," I mumbled to myself as I walked the two waters back to the table.

"Here you go," I said to no one in particular and walked back to the kitchen to do some more mental calculations. Maybe I could ask the landlord if I could pay the rent a little late, I thought. Then I could borrow my rent money to fix my car. I sighed as I thought about approaching my mean-faced landlord. I had a feeling she wasn't going to go to be happy if I asked her if I could pay my rent slightly late.

"You okay, Lucky?" Mike peered at me from his station and I nodded quickly.

I didn't want to get Mike and Shayla involved with my problems. I knew they would want to loan me the money, but I also knew that they had two kids to support and they were barely able to do that themselves.

"Yeah. Thanks, Mike."

"What did Mike do now?" Shayla came back into the kitchen and looked Mike up and down. "You bothering my girl?"

"No, Shay. Lucky's just looking slightly down."

"Oh, I'm sorry, girl, maybe they won't be as cheap as they look." Shayla grinned at me as she talked about the new couple that had been seated in my area. Everyone who worked at Lou's knew from the moment they approached the table what sort of tip was going to be forthcoming. Anytime a young couple came in all lovey-dovey usually meant a low tip.

"I'm sure they will be." I laughed. "They are sharing their entrée."

"Oh, man." Shayla shook her head and patted my shoulder to show her condolences. "But at least you have Mr. Rich. He should be good for a few dollars, right?"

"Yeah. He always tips well." I smiled and looked out into the dining room to make sure none of my customers was looking around for me. I stared at Zane Beaumont again and I noticed that he kept his hands to his side of the table. I always saw his dates with their hands stretched out and inching towards him, but I never saw him holding hands with them. I wondered if he had slept with them all. He was certainly good-looking enough to bag any girl he wanted. I wondered if he dumped them as soon as they said yes. I wouldn't have been surprised to find out he was a kick-em-out-the-next-morning sort of guy. I shook my head and grinned to myself. He was a spend-the-night-at-their-place-and-leave-early-in-the-morning sort of guy. I was positive of it.

"What's so funny, Lucky?"

"Just wondering if Mr. Rich is as good in bed as he looks," I said wryly and turned to Shayla with a grin. "And don't you dare say a word."

"Girl, I'm not going to say anything." She winked at me and laughed. "But I'm betting that is a man who can go all night long."

"Okay, I'm out of here," I groaned and ran back into the dining room. I didn't want to think about Zane and sex. It had been too long since I'd dated or had sex, and just thinking about him was getting me hot and bothered. But it had been my decision, and I needed to remember that. I couldn't afford to daydream about a guy like Zane.

"Everything okay, Lucky?" Zane's voice was deep and husky, and he looked at me with concern. "I hope nothing's burning in the kitchen."

"Oh, no. It's all good." I smiled at him and turned away from his gaze. Every time he said my name, I felt a flush inside. "Do you guys need anything else?"

"Just the check." His smile was gone and his eyes were vacant again. "And quickly, please."

"Sure." I turned away, confused by his sudden change in demeanor. "I'll get it right now."

"So, Zane, where are we going now?" his date preened.

"I thought we could go get some cocktails on the beach."

"South Beach?"

"Yeah, we can go to Washington. I know a cool place."

"We can go to my place."

"Yeah, we can do that." His voice was smooth as silk. I peeked behind my shoulder and watched as he caressed her hand. *Asshole!* I thought to myself as I printed out Zane's check. I wanted to slap myself for thinking that perhaps he wasn't the playboy I had thought him to be. He obviously was. He was not boyfriend material, and I had to keep reminding myself of that.

"Here you go." I dropped the check off at the table and spoke to the girl, ignoring Zane. "You can pay at the front."

I walked back to the kitchen quickly and into the bathroom. I locked the door and quickly splashed some water on my heated face. I was upset and frustrated. I stared in the mirror at my dark brown hair and brushed my fingers through my ponytail. I gazed into my wide, upset eyes through the mirror and saw the stress lines at the corners and sighed. I looked depressed and washed out; I couldn't even compare to the bevy of girls Zane paraded in and out of the restaurant. Sometimes living in Miami gives me an inferiority complex, and I'm not one prone to low self-esteem. Don't get me wrong, I have my days like everyone else, but generally I'm happy with my looks and my life. I'm not Miss America, but I don't think I'm ugly. I didn't like the uneasy feeling in my stomach. I didn't really understand why I was so upset at Zane's dismissiveness. It wasn't like we were friends or anything, and it wasn't as if I liked him. I mean, yes, I'll admit it, I thought he was cute, but he wasn't all that. And he was a player and he was pompous. The typical rich, handsome guy who's had everything handed to him. He wasn't the type of guy I wanted to end up with. No, not at all. I just had to keep reminding myself of that.

"Lucky, you there?" Shayla banged on the door.

"Yeah, I'll be right out."

"You better, your young man is waiting outside for you."

"What young …?" *Oh, shit*, I thought. He was probably mad I gave the check to the girl. My heart started thumping and I felt a little sick. What if he decided he wasn't going to come back to this diner? What if I never saw him again?

"Thanks, Shayla." I walked out of the bathroom and through the kitchen to the front of the store where Zane was waiting for me with a concerned expression on his face.

"Hey, Lucky, thanks for coming over to talk before I left." His blue eyes pierced mine and I stared back at him without a smile.

"Sure."

"I have to go in a second because she's waiting in the car."

"Okay." I wanted to ask him why he called her "she" instead of by her name. "So did I get something wrong on the bill or something?"

"I wanted to apologize if I said anything to upset you." He paused. "I just hope I didn't come off as rude."

"Oh, no, of course not." I was taken aback at his statement.

"I was raised to treat everyone equally," he continued, and I looked at him in surprise. What was he talking about? "I hope you don't think I was disrespecting you're a waitress?"

"Not at all." I blushed and looked away. All he saw when he looked at me was a waitress. I wanted to laugh. Even if I didn't have my rules, he wouldn't be interested in me.

"Good. Well, have a pleasant evening, Lucky."

"You too." I smiled at him weakly.

"Oh, I intend to." He grinned at me and then sauntered out the door after rubbing my shoulder.

I went back to his table to collect the cash he had left on it for my tip. My jaw dropped when I saw the hundred-dollar bill and a short "sorry" message written on a napkin. I looked back to the front of the restaurant and sighed. I stuffed the bill into my pocket and walked back to the kitchen with my head starting to pound. I was so confused and felt almost delirious. I touched the spot on my shoulder he had rubbed, and I felt a warm flush run through my body as I remembered his warm touch. I shook my head at the excited feeling that was running through my veins. "Remember the rules, Lucky," I muttered to myself as I started on my side work duties.

CHAPTER TWO

"LUCKY, COME TO THIS party with us tonight," Leeza begged me as I walked into the kitchen, yawning on Saturday morning.

"I'm working tonight."

"Come after work."

"I'll be too tired."

"Come on, Lucky," she pleaded. "You haven't hung out in ages."

"Leeza, you know I'm not in the mood for partying." I sighed.

"It's not a frat party," she whined. "This girl I met in Econ is dating a DJ and he has a hookup on Star Island and some hotshot actor is holding a party to celebrate his new movie being number one or something."

"What actor?" I asked curiously.

"I don't know, but I'm sure there will be lots of hot guys there."

"I don't care about hot guys," I sighed.

"You might be a nun now, Lucky, but that doesn't mean you have to miss out on every piece of fun in the universe." Leeza flung her long, blonde hair over her shoulders and shook her head. "We're only young once, so let's have some fun."

"I'm not going to meet the guy I'm looking for at a snooty party."

"You might."

"In between the potheads and the cokeheads?"

"Since when did you become so judgmental?"

"Since I decided I wanted a good guy who was going to value me."

"Yawn." Leeza drank some freshly squeezed orange juice and rolled her eyes. "Just try and come, please, Lucky. You know you, me, and Shannon haven't hung out in ages."

"It's a girls' night?" I squinted at her suspiciously.

"Yes!" she beamed at me innocently, and I sighed, knowing that if I saw her alone for five minutes, I would be shocked.

"Okay, I'll try."

It would help stop my dreams of Zane Beaumont, at least. That guy was seriously doing a number on my head. He intrigued me and I was starting to have too many naughty dreams of him doing things to me that I'd only seen in movies.

"Wear something cute tonight, Lucky." Leeza grinned at me and ran out of the kitchen. "Have fun at work today. I'm going to the beach to get my tan on."

"Lucky!" I called out to her enviously, and she laughed.

"No need to say your name, girl."

"Ha ha."

I opened the fridge as she ran to her room and looked for something to eat. I wanted to make sure I ate something hearty before I got ready for work. Lou's Burger Joint gave us a fifty-percent percent discount on all of our purchases, but I knew I had no money to spare until after I got my car fixed. I looked at the rotting head of lettuce and the dried out chicken breasts I had cooked a few days before and sighed. I wrinkled my nose and opened the freezer and grabbed the Hot Pockets quickly. I knew they weren't mine, but I also knew Leeza wouldn't mind if I ate one. As soon as the microwave beeped, I grabbed the Hot Pocket in a napkin and ran back up to my room to count my cash. I nearly had enough to get my car fixed now. I had thought about applying for a credit card to pay for it until I got the cash, but then I remembered how easy it was for people to get themselves into credit card debt. I watched Suze Orman on TV religiously; I knew what bad news credit cards could be to someone my age. I already had enough financial issues; I didn't need to add any more to the mix.

I lay back on my bed and stretched out. It seemed as if nothing was going right in my life. Or at least, nothing that I wanted to go right. I hated being single. I needed to take proactive measures to find a new guy—one who would fit what I was looking for. I turned on my clock radio, sang along to the latest Britney song, and wondered how it was so easy for some people to find a guy to settle down with and why it was so hard for me. I was starting to feel like a bit of a loser. I knew I was pretty and smart but that didn't really seem to be getting me anywhere.

I jumped up as I realized the time. I had to be at work in about thirty minutes, and I wasn't even nearly ready. I felt like my life was already too monotonous. All I ever seemed to do was go to work and go to school. It was starting to feel tedious and boring, and I was glad I had decided to attend the party with Leeza this evening. I needed something to take me out of my normal routine; I just needed to remember that I wasn't there to partake in the craziness but to have a little fun.

I was tired when I got out of work, and I drove home, feeling depressed. I had made barely any money and didn't feel like going to the party anymore, but I knew Leeza and Shannon would be disappointed if I didn't show up. Leeza had called me on my break to make sure I was coming. She had sounded so excited that I was finally going to be spending an evening out with them like we had in the past that I felt too guilty to say no. I knew I definitely had to go when I saw an emerald green dress on my bed with a note from Leeza saying she had bought it for me as a gift.

I sighed as I walked into the door at the party. I was overwhelmed by the number of people and cars and I briefly considered leaving and going back home. The house was packed with a lot of people I didn't know, and a lot of people I couldn't afford to know. I pulled up the driveway in between a Rolls Royce and a Bentley, and I felt out of place before I had even gotten out of my car. I looked around to see if I could spot Leeza, and I gasped when I saw Zane Beaumont talking animatedly to a guy who looked very familiar. I continued to stare at them, trying to figure out who the other guy was, when Zane turned around. He must have felt my eyes boring into him because he looked directly at me. His expression changed quickly and ran the gamut of surprised, happy, and upset.   I turned around with my heart beating fast when I saw him frown and then walk away quickly. What was Zane doing here? I quickly grabbed a champagne flute from one of the waiters' trays and gulped it down, hoping it would give me some liquid courage for the night. I couldn't believe Zane was at the party. My whole body had felt alive when we'd made eye contact, and I was glad that it was so dark that he couldn't have seen my face flushing.

"Lucky?" I heard his voice and tried not to flinch as he touched me on the shoulder.

"Hi." I turned around slowly and tried to avoid his eyes as I smiled quickly.

"I thought that was you." He frowned as he looked me up and down. "You look different."

"Yeah. I'm in a dress," I quipped. "And I have on makeup that hasn't melted off yet."

"And your hair is down." He reached over and touched it. "It's so soft and silky."

"Thanks to Chi," I joked, and cursed myself inwardly. He probably didn't even know what Chi was. "I have naturally curly hair, so I use it to calm down the frizz and straighten it," I explained to him, wanting to kick myself at how boring I was being.

"I see." He nodded, looking as though he had no clue as to what I was talking about.

"You should see it when it's curly. It's crazy."

"Well, I can't tell."

"I'm like the frizz monster." I giggled nervously. *Play it cool, Lucky.* I took a deep breath and tried again. "You're lucky your hair is always so straight and silky naturally." I wanted to slap myself as soon as the words were out of my mouth. "I mean, that's how it looks now, not in the past. I never noticed in the past."

"Thanks." He laughed.

"Do you use any special products?" Stop talking about hair care, Lucky!

"No. I use Head and Shoulders shampoo and conditioner, and that's about it."

"Aw." I looked around the room with a red face and waved my hands. "This is a really cool party, huh?"

"It's okay." He shrugged. "I didn't know you knew Mike."

"Who?"

"Mike Vegara. The guy throwing this party."

"Oh, I don't." I bit my lip. "My friend invited me. Don't tell anyone, but I wasn't really invited. I'm not really part of this crowd."

"What crowd?"

"The rich and famous crowd." And then I remembered how Zane knew me. "Well, you know that already." I let out a weak laugh, "I wouldn't be working at Lou's if I was rich and made of money."

"Then I'm glad you're not rich." He smiled, a gigantic toothy smile, and I couldn't stop myself from grinning back at him. "Because I feel sorry for anyone who is a part of this crowd."

"Oh?" I looked at him in surprise.

"It's a long story." He sighed. "I don't want to bore you."

"I don't think you have a boring bone in your body." *Why was I so obvious?* I wanted to pinch myself.

"There are many girls who would beg to differ with you there." He laughed.

"So who's your date tonight?" I questioned, looking around.

"No date tonight." He laughed.

I wiggled my eyebrows in surprised. "That's got to be a first."

"I usually reserve Fridays for my dates." He stared into my eyes. "I think you've met every woman I've taken out in the last few months."

"A different one every week." I laughed, trying not to let my curiosity get the better of me. I wanted to know why he dated so many different women, but I knew it was none of my business.

"Well, I have to get what I need." He cleared his throat. "More importantly, don't ever take Friday nights off. I'm not sure my dates would go as well if you weren't there."

"I'm not sure I'm a good luck charm. I never see you with the same girl more than once." I hoped he would pick up the hint and answer my unasked question.

"What about you? You here with your boyfriend?" His eyes bore into mine intently. Even in the darkness of the room, his eyes sparkled a vivid blue.

"No." For some reason, I didn't want to tell him that I didn't have a boyfriend. I didn't want him to know that since he had been frequenting Lou's, he was all I could think about.

"I'm surprised he let you come out by yourself," he continued, trying to fish an answer out of me.

"I'm here with friends." I smiled and looked around nervously.

"So what does he do?" he persisted, and I wondered why it was so important for him to know.

"Who?" I frowned, pretending to be confused.

"Your boyfriend."

"Oh, well, I don't exactly have one right now."

"Aw, you're rocking the single life?" He grinned and moved in closer to me.

"You could say that." I rolled my eyes.

"You're a beautiful girl, I'm sure there has to be someone you're interested in."

"Not really." Just you, and you're a player, so no thanks, I thought to myself.

"This isn't the sort of party to meet a good guy, though." Zane spoke seriously. "I mean, a lot of the guys here aren't the sort I would recommend to a girl like you."

"Well, I will try and remember that." I was unsure if his comment was meant to be helpful or disparaging.

"I'm sure you'll meet a Mr. Wonderful soon." He paused. "I guess that's what you women want, right? A Mr. Wonderful to sweep you off your feet and promise you a forever?"

"You could say that," I answered honestly. "Though I'm waiting patiently. I know the right guy is out there somewhere." I'm hoping he'll come sooner rather than later, but there was no way I was going to tell him that.

"So, Lucky. What else do you do aside from working at Lou's?"

"I'm studying history at UM. I know it sounds a bit boring, but I love it."

"History, huh?" His eyes glowed. "Know anything about the Civil Rights Era?"

"It's my specialty, actually." I spoke enthusiastically. "I'm actually focusing on that period of time for my thesis."

"I can tell you enjoy it." He smiled gently and reached over and stroked my cheek softly. "There's something wonderful about a woman who is passionate about something."

"I'm a ..." My breath caught and my cheek burned under his touch.

"Lucky, there you are." Leeza ran up to me and squealed. "I was so worried you weren't going to come."

"I'm here." I smiled and did a little twirl. I saw Zane laugh at my little dance and I smiled back at him warmly.

"I want you to meet this guy." She grabbed my arm enthusiastically.

"I'm actually talking to someone." I smiled at Zane apologetically, and he grinned back at me.

"Oh?" Leeza turned around and stared at Zane, her blue eyes nearly popping out as she looked him up and down. "Hi, I'm Leeza, Lucky's best friend. And you are?" She flung her blonde hair over her shoulders, and it took everything I had to smile and not roll my eyes. She was a shameless flirt and she never met a man she didn't want to make fall under her spell.

"Zane." He smiled at Leeza briefly and then looked at me. "I'm a friend of Lucky's."

"You never told me about any Zane." Leeza stared at me with accusatory eyes.

"Well, we've just been getting to know each other recently," I started.

"Now, now, Lucky." Zane slid his arm around my waist. "What do you consider the last three months? The honeymoon period?"

"Well, you know." I was left speechless by his little act, and his hand lit a fiery trail on my back as he moved it back and forth.

"You two are dating?" Leeza hissed. "You have got to be joking."

"Why?" Zane questioned her. "Did Lucky not tell you about our marathon sessions in the bedroom? I think we nearly broke her bed the other evening."

"Zane." I laughed and hit him in the arm. "Leeza's my roommate."

"Well, darn it. It was worth a try." He grinned at me and his nose brushed mine as he leaned in to talk to me. For the next few seconds, we just stared at each other, and all I wanted was for him to kiss me.

"It was good seeing you, Lucky. Have a good evening."

Zane pulled away from me slowly and I felt that sharp sting of regret that I hadn't moved in for the kiss. Before I could say anything, he turned around and disappeared back into the crowd. I felt disappointed but tried to hide my frustration as I turned back to Leeza. It was probably better that I didn't spend too much time getting to know Zane better; I didn't want to end up as one of his Friday night dates.

"He was cute." Leeza grinned. "But he seems like a psycho."

"Why does he seem like a psycho?"

"I don't know. Just something about him seemed off. And his crappy joke."

"He's a nice—"

"Come on, Lucky, let me introduce you to Evan." Leeza cut me off and flung her hair over her shoulder again. She was wearing a super-tight black mini dress and I was slightly worried that her boobs were going to pop out each time she flung her hair.

"Who's Evan?" I asked disinterestedly. I looked around the room to see if I could find where Zane had gone.

"Just come." She grabbed my arm and pushed through the crowds of trendy people until we got to the stairs and then she let go. "All the cool guys are hanging out in the music room."

"Uh, okay?" I frowned. "Isn't the party at the bottom of the stairs, though?"

"Don't be a buzz kill, Lucky. Everyone knows the best parts of a party don't occur in the public part of the party. All the cool people like Evan hang out separately."

"I'm not cool and I don't want a cool guy," I sighed.

"I'm sure you will like Evan," Leeza pleaded.

"Leeza, I'm really not in the mood for this."

"He's a hottie and he's rich."

"Leeza, you know I'm not looking for—"

"Just give him a chance, Lucky. Your plan hasn't exactly been working for you. I haven't seen you on a date in months. And I don't even think you have a vibrator. Just give him a chance, okay?"

I didn't stop to correct her comment. It wasn't like I wanted to scream out to the world, "I haven't had sex in over a year!" I knew that wouldn't help my case. I tried to forget about Zane as I followed Leeza upstairs. I wished I had a potion to stop my heart from racing every time I saw him. I could close my eyes and picture his sky blue irises staring into mine. They always seemed so open and honest. But I knew he was a player—a man not to be trusted. I just wished that I could embed that information into my heart. But every week that he came into the diner, was a week where I found myself liking him more and more. It was funny. I was his server and we weren't really friends, but we had had some pretty interesting conversations in the diner. Sometimes they happened while he waited on a date to arrive, and sometimes he stayed in the restaurant and chatted for a bit if the girl decided to take a cab home. Getting to know Zane these last few months had really brightened my day, and I couldn't imagine a Friday night without him coming in.

"Come on, Lucky!" Leeza called down the stairs as I walked up slowly to meet her. "Hurry it up, I don't have all night."

"I'm coming," I sighed.

"Come on." She grabbed my arm as I reached the top of the stairs and then pulled me into a room with her. "This is my friend Lucky, everyone." Leeza's tone changed as she opened the door, and I followed her in hesitantly.

There were four guys sitting in chairs drinking, and they all smirked at me as they looked me over.

"Lucky, this is Evan." She pointed to a tall guy with jet-black hair and striking green eyes.

"Hi." I shook his hand, and he leaned over to kiss me.

"Hi, beautiful."

I blushed at his words and turned away, slightly uncomfortable. I saw another guy in the corner of the room giving me a sympathetic look, and he jumped up.

"Lay off, Evan." He hit Evan on the shoulder and held his hand out to me. "Hi, I'm Braydon."

"Hi, I'm Lucky." I smiled, grateful that I didn't have to deal with Evan. Leeza had disappeared, and I was already feeling slightly annoyed.

"That's an unusual name." Braydon laughed. "Would you like a drink?"

"I'm okay, thanks. I have to drive home, so I'm not having anything else."

"Well, that's no fun." He grinned.

"Sorry, I guess I'm not a fun person." I grinned back and made to turn around, but he grabbed me by the arm.

"Hey, Lucky, want to have a seat?"

"Yeah. Thanks." I followed him back to the corner, and we sat on a brown leather couch.

"So tell me about your name, Lucky." He smiled a genuine boyish smile.

I relaxed as I looked into his brown eyes. He seemed like a nice guy, somewhat familiar, but I knew I'd never met him before.

"My parents thought they couldn't conceive. They tried for years." I smiled. "And then they had me. And they considered themselves the luckiest parents in the world."

"Wow, that must have been a nice surprise."

"Yeah. They were really happy to have me." I smiled wistfully. "They used to tell people that they'd won the lottery. And then they would boast about how they were the luckiest people in the world."

"Well, I bet they are." He smiled at me gently, though I noticed his eyes were slightly glazed.

"Yeah." I let my voice drift off as I felt tears pricking my eyes. I didn't want to be talking about this right now. "So how did you get the name Braydon? It's not that common either."

"My mother made it up." He laughed and ran his hands over his bald head. "She wanted a name that no other kid had. So she made up Braydon."

"It's a cool name."

"A cool name for an uncool guy." He laughed modestly.

I stared at him as he laughed, and I was about to say something when I realized that he looked really, really familiar. "Hey, do I know you?" I cocked my head, trying to think where I knew him. "I don't think I do, but there is something about your face."

"Aw, drat, you finally figured it out." He shook his head, and I saw a red flush across his cheeks. "I'm Braydon Eagle."

"Um, okay?" I paused, not really sure what I was supposed to have figured out.

"You still don't know, do you?" He laughed and looked amused.

"No, sorry." I bit my lip and flushed, embarrassed that I had no clue.

"That's okay. I had to shave my hair off last week. Imagine me with a full head of bleached blond hair."

"Oh, my God!" I looked at him in surprise. "You're Braydon Eagle." I felt my cheeks heat up. He was the famous actor Braydon Eagle. He had been a child star and had recently hit it big in movies. Hollywood called him the new Leonardo DiCaprio. I had even had a poster of him on my wall when I was in grade school.

"Don't tell anyone, though." He laughed and ran his hand over his head again.

"You look truly different without the hair."

"I know. I'm trying to get used to it myself." He laughed self-consciously. "No one's mistaking me for a surfer now."

"At least you can be incognito."

"That's always nice at parties like these."

"I would have thought you enjoyed all the attention."

"Not really." He laughed. "Well, I used to. Now, not so much. I've had enough of the Hollywood life."

"I'm surprised anyone could have enough of that." I smiled and leaned back into the chair comfortably. "I don't know many guys who would say that."

"It's about quality and not quantity." He laughed. "Listen to me. I sound like a douche, don't I?"

"Not at all," I said honestly.

"Hey, Lucky, am I going to get lucky tonight?" Evan shouted from across the room, and I blushed uncomfortably.

"Shut up, Evan." Braydon shook his head and leaned into me.

"You got anything, Braydon? My man here is looking to score."

"Evan, stop smoking the weed. I have no idea what you're talking about." Braydon rolled his eyes and leaned towards me. "Ignore him. He's just being an ass."

"Thanks." I smiled gratefully. "Though that's not the first time I've heard that *witty* comment. I don't know why guys think they are the first ones to come up with the 'getting lucky tonight' comment."

"Hopefully not all of them were as annoying as Evan."

"Not all." I grinned, and Braydon laughed.

"So, what do you do for a living, Lucky?"

"I'm in college, and I work."

"Oh, yeah? Where do you go to school?"

"University of Miami."

"Nice. I was thinking of applying there."

"Really?" I looked at him in disbelief.

"Well, kind of." He laughed. "I was going to be in the remake of *Miami Vice*, but they decided to postpone the series, and then I decided to make the leap from TV to films. But it's always good to have something to fall back on. You can't have enough money."

"Oh, okay." I wanted to pinch myself to make sure I wasn't imagining anything. The whole situation felt surreal. I couldn't quite believe that I was in a room, sitting on a couch with Braydon Eagle, one of the hottest young stars in Hollywood. Things like this just didn't happen to me.

"What are you studying?"

"History." I laughed at the expression on his face. "Don't worry, I'm not going to quiz you."

"Thanks. I can barely remember our current president's name. Don't ask me anyone else's."

"That's okay. I don't think history is a popular subject." I smiled.

"So when do you graduate?"

"Next year, I hope." I laughed.

"And what's next?"

"No idea."

"Well, you still have time."

"Yeah." I ran my hands through my hair and grimaced as I felt the frizzy waves. *So much for my straight tresses*, I thought. The humidity had taken care of that.

"Do you think you'll be a teacher?" Braydon continued. "I've always seen myself marrying a teacher."

I didn't quite know how to answer his question and tried to formulate a response in my mind before the door opened.

"Hey, y'all. We're here." A tall, leggy blonde walked into the room giggling, and I watched her curiously. She was beautiful. Maybe one of the most beautiful women I had ever seen in my life.

"What's up, Angelique?" Evan whistled at her, and she giggled again.

"Nada. Zane and I want to get this party started." I froze at her words and looked towards the door and saw Zane standing there. He had a beer in his hand, and the top buttons of his white shirt were undone.

"Yo, bro, what up?" Evan jumped up and fist-bumped him.

"Not much. What's happening, Evan?" Zane didn't smile as he spoke nonchalantly. He looked relaxed, but I could sense a weird tension coming from him.

"Come on, Zane." The blonde grabbed his arm and pulled him into the room. I felt a dart of jealousy as he allowed her to guide him in further. I turned away, and looked at Braydon and smiled.

"I have been thinking about teaching or going to grad school."

"Awesome. I've always wondered …" I knew that Braydon was still talking, but I could feel Zane's eyes on me. My body froze, and I moved my face slightly to look at him. He studied me on the couch with Braydon and nodded before turning away from me, and I felt my face flush with confusion.

"Yeah." I nodded at Braydon without even bothering to ask him what he had just said.

He laughed. "You haven't heard a word I just said, have you?"

I shook my head, feeling guilty, and he laughed even harder. "Lucky, you are a real refreshment to me right now."

"Uh, thanks." I smiled quickly, not actually sure what he meant.

"I would love to take you out some time."

"Oh." I blushed, unsure of what to say in response. To avoid answering right away, I decided to straighten out my dress.

"Braydon Eagle, you sly dog." The blonde ran up to the couch and sat on his lap. "I didn't know you were here."

"Hi, Angelique." He smiled and rolled his eyes.

"Why didn't you call me back? I wanted you to come pregame with us."

"I'm here now."

"Didn't you miss me?" She pouted and ran her finger across his cheek. I sat there uncomfortably and started to get up.

"Angelique, you're making Lucky uncomfortable." Braydon pushed her off of his lap, and she looked at me with distaste.

"I'm okay." I attempted a smile, but Angelique flicked her hair and called to Zane.

"Zane, Braydon's being rude."

"I'm sure he is." Zane walked up to Angelique and put his arm around her.

"Yes, he was," she pouted. "Do something about it."

"Don't worry, I'm trying to," Zane mumbled under his breath, and I stared up at him. He frowned at me, and I could sense that he was unhappy with me for some reason. We continued to stare at each other and I saw Braydon look back and forth at us.

"Do you two know each other?" His tone sounded odd.

"Yes," I said at the same time Zane said, "No."

My feelings were hurt that he pretended not to know me and I looked away from him and stared across the room."

"Hello, Braydon." Zane's voice was brusque as he acknowledged Braydon.

"Zane." Braydon nodded, and I watched them both curiously as a silent message seemed to pass between them.

"Zane. Let's go in the hot tub. Braydon, why don't you join us?"

"I'm having a conversation, Angelique." Braydon spoke to Angelique, but he looked at Zane.

"I'm sure she won't mind." Her voice sounded sharp, and I felt Braydon's hand grab hold of mine.

"Angelique, why don't you and Zane go?"

"Don't want me to interrupt your conversation with Lucky?" Zane's voice was smooth with a slight undertone.

"What do you care?" Braydon frowned and gave him a challenging look.

"I don't." Zane's voice was sharp and seemed to send Braydon a message.

"We met at the restaurant I work at," I interjected into the conversation, trying to let Braydon know I wasn't one of Zane's many girls.

"You work at a restaurant?" Angelique looked at me disdainfully, and I could feel the dislike emanating from her eyes. She obviously didn't like the attention being away from her.

"Come on, Angelique." Zane pulled her away before staring at me for a few seconds. I watched as they walked across the room and exited, and I tried to exhale the disappointment that resonated through my body.

"Sorry about Angelique, she can be a bit of a bitch." Braydon sidled up next to me and placed his arm around me.

"That's okay." I smiled briefly and tried to shift away from him slightly. "How do you know Zane?" I asked him curiously.

"Zane?" Braydon looked at me with a funny look in his eye. "I don't honestly know him that well. I was friends with his brother."

"Oh?"

"Yeah. But I met them both through his dad."

"His dad?"

"Yeah, his dad is Jeff Beaumont, the head of Paragon Studios."

"Oh, wow." I felt faint at his words. So I had been right. Zane was a spoiled rich boy. Only he was richer than I had even imagined. No wonder he dated so many different women. He had the world at his feet.

"You didn't know?" Braydon shook his head in disbelief. "You really are one-of-a-kind."

"Thanks, I think." I laughed, and Braydon joined in.

"Can I take you to lunch tomorrow, Lucky?"

"I, uh, don't know."

"I promise not to bite." He held up some fingers. "Scout's honor."

"You were a scout?" I looked at him in surprise.

"No, but I played one in a movie when I was a kid." He laughed.

I shook my head, feeling drawn to his boyish charm. "Well, I guess that's close enough."

"So, tomorrow?" He looked at me earnestly. "I know you don't know me from Adam, but really, I'm a nice guy. I know most actors are portrayed as assholes and players, but I'm not one of those guys." He shook his head and grinned. "I feel like an idiot for just saying that."

"Don't." I stared into his eyes and nodded. "I'll go to lunch with you."

"Yes!" He fist pumped and ran his hand over his head again. "Let me get your number and I'll call you in the morning."

"Okay." I smiled shyly, gave him my number, and then paused for a moment to think about everything. I wasn't sure if Braydon was going to have all the qualities I was looking for, but I knew it was time to start dating again to find that perfect guy. I knew I couldn't keep fantasizing about Zane. There was no way I could compete with someone like Angelique.

"Awesome." He jumped up and grabbed my hands to pull me up. "Now, let's go dance and have some fun."

***

It was two a.m. when I finally left the party. Braydon had practically begged me to stay the night, and he had even offered to share his bed with me. I had been flattered, but I had stayed firm with my "nos." I had seen Zane watching us as we danced around the room and I felt self-conscious at his stares.

I had half-hoped that he would cut in and ask me for a dance, but he never did.

I was grinning as I walked to my car and realized that I was truly happy that Leeza had invited me to the party, even though I hadn't seen her since that earlier appearance. Braydon seemed to be a really nice and fun guy, and I almost forgot he was a movie star as we danced around the room. Everything about the night had been perfect. Well, almost perfect. I had seen Zane a few more times throughout the night, and he had just stared at me blankly and a little coldly. It had made me feel uncomfortable and upset. Part of me wasn't sure why he looked so displeased with me. Was he upset that I was hanging out with all his rich friends even though I was just a lowly waitress? I had tried to make eye contact with him and smile, but he had just remained stoic and looked away from me every time. I tried to dismiss the hurt that coursed through my veins at his look, but I couldn't quite eradicate the feeling.

"Don't think about it, Lucky," I muttered to myself as I drove back to my apartment. I groaned as my car started making a funny noise and nearly burst out in tears as I heard the engine die. As I pulled it over to the side of the road, it stopped. I sat behind the wheel, unsure of what to do, when I saw the lights of another car pull up behind me. *Oh, shit.* I thought to myself as I saw a figure get out of the car and walk up towards me. I checked to make sure my doors were locked and bit my lip hard. "Please don't kill me, please don't kill me." I closed my eyes briefly and nearly screamed as I heard the knock on the window. I peered through the window and rolled it down slowly. I was shocked to see Zane's face staring back at me.

"Everything okay, Lucky?" His words seemed unduly harsh, but his eyes were worried. As I stared at him, I wondered how he just happened to be behind me as I broke down. I nodded my head slowly, slightly confused as to my feelings of seeing him there. I kept my mouth closed because I was unwilling to speak. I had a feeling that my voice was going to be too squeaky, and I didn't want him to see how scared I had been.

"Did your car break down?" he asked again, and I nodded again, staring at his pink lips. I swallowed hard as I imagined what it would feel like to have his lips pressed against mine.

"Do you need me to jump your car?" he asked at the same time I asked, "Were you following me?"

CHAPTER THREE

"CAN YOU GET OUT OF THE CAR, Lucky?" Zane's voice sounded harsh, and he looked furious. I was a little worried he was going to scold me for something I had no control over. The look on his face reminded me of my father's when I was a little kid and had done something wrong.

"I can, but I'm not sure I will," I quipped, trying to change the mood. When he didn't respond, I quickly changed my own tone. "But don't try and change the subject. Were you following me?"

"Of course not." His voice was aloof as he opened the door. "Get out of the car, Lucky, and let me see what's going on."

"I can check myself, you know," I spat back, annoyed at his attitude and slightly disappointed.

"Lucky." His tone rose.

"My head gasket is gone," I sighed as I climbed out of the car.

"How do you know?" He looked surprised to hear me using a mechanical term.

"Because I knew it was going," I sighed again and looked up at him. His face was dark in the moonlight, and he still looked furious as he stared back at me.

"Are you telling me that you knew that your head gasket was gone, but you still decided to drive?" His voice rose. "And you still went to a party by yourself and thought it was smart to leave in the early hours of the morning?"

I nodded, slightly scared to answer him.

"Of all the irresponsible things to do, Lucky!" he shouted. "I thought you were smarter than that. Can you imagine how your parents would feel if they received a phone call from a cop about your car breaking down and you being attacked or killed?"

"I think you're being a little over the top, Zane." I frowned. "I'm a big girl, I can take care of myself."

"So what would you be doing right now then?" He tapped his foot and leaned back against my car. He looked like a smug bastard, and I felt ashamed of myself for allowing my heart to race as I stared at him. He was one sexy asshole, that was for sure.

"Are you going to help me or what?" I snapped.

"Oh, so now you want my help?"

"Actually, what I want is to know how you happened to be behind me when I broke down in the middle of the night."

"It doesn't matter." He sighed, and bending down, he pulled the keys out of my ignition. "Do you have everything you need from your car?"

"Yes. Why?"

"Because I'm going to take you home."

"I'm not going anywhere with you."

"Just let me take you home." He sighed.

"What about my car?" I protested. "I can't leave my car here. I need it."

"We can call a tow truck driver to come pick it up," he said calmly. The low tone of his voice was in direct contrast to my screeches.

"How much is that going to cost?"

"I'm not sure? Maybe a hundred and fifty? I'm sure there will be an extra charge for it being the middle of the night."

"One hundred and fifty," I sighed heavily.

How was I going to pay for the tow truck driver and get my car fixed? It just wasn't going to happen. Not with the amount of money I had in my account. How was I going to get to work and school? Everything was falling apart around me, and I felt as if I was going to start hyperventilating.

"I found a local tow truck number. I can call them now." Zane peered at me with a worried expression as he looked up from his phone. "Do you know where you want the car towed to?"

"Can't they just take it to a garage?"

"Which one?"

"I don't know," I sighed. "I can't afford to get it fixed right away."

"Oh." He looked at me with concern in his voice, and I turned away because I didn't want to see pity in his eyes. "Can you ask your parents to loan you the money?"

"No." My voice was curt. "Can you give me a ride home, please?"

"How will you get to your car?"

"I'll get a ride." I bit my lip. What if Shannon and Leeza didn't answer their phones or come home? How would I get back to my car in the morning?

"How about you stay over at my place, and tomorrow morning we figure out what to do with your car?"

"I don't know." I looked away, unsure of what to say.

"I promise I won't bite." He grinned mischievously.

"That's not a worry I have."

"Unless you want me to bite, of course."

"No, thanks."

"I guess vampires aren't cool now?"

"Vampires?" I frowned, wondering if he was high or something.

"Isn't *Twilight* all the craze? Don't all you girls love that Edward Pattinson guy or something?"

I burst out laughing, and he watched me as tears rolled out of my eyes.

"Edward Pattinson, ha ha ha." I couldn't control myself, and Zane stood there, staring at me with a bemused expression on his face.

"Did I say something funny?"

"His name is Robert Pattinson, he played the character Edward Cullen, and no, I'm not a huge fan. Well, I'm a slight fan, or I was when I was in high school, but no, that doesn't mean I want a guy who is a vampire."

"Because they exist?"

"Who exists?"

"Vampires."

"No, they don't exist."

"So then it doesn't matter if you want one or not then."

"I was just answering your question," I said, infuriated at him. "You were the one who brought them up in the first place."

"So is it a yes or a no?"

"Is what a yes or a no?" I said, thoroughly confused at this point.

"Do you want me to bite you?" He leaned towards me, and his eyes were sparkling. I held my breath as his lips came within inches of mine. I was scared that he was going to kiss me, but I knew I wouldn't pull away if he did. I closed my eyes and waited to feel his lips to press against mine. I could feel the warmth of his breath against my cheek, and my heart started pounding, excited at what was about to happen. I waited patiently for about several seconds, and then opened my eyes to see what was going on, as I hadn't felt his lips press against mine yet.

As I opened my eyes, I saw that Zane was staring at me with an indescribable look on his face. I saw several emotions flicker through his eyes quickly, and the look was so intense that my breath caught. We stared at each other for a while, and then he looked away.

"Let's go." He grabbed my hand and led me back to his car, and I followed, silently confused. I knew we had just had a moment, but I didn't understand it. I wanted to ask why he hadn't kissed me. My whole body was still on edge, waiting for the meeting of our lips.

"You didn't kiss me," I blurted out as I got into the car. He looked at me with a surprised expression. His what-the-fuck expression matched the screaming in my head. I was shocked and horrified that I had spoken the words in my head out loud.

"I didn't think it was a good idea," he said, slowly starting the car.

"Why?" I continued, not really sure what I was hoping he would say.

"I'm not looking for a relationship, Lucky. I don't think it would be a good idea for us to hook up."

"A kiss isn't a hookup." I felt my stomach fold over at his words. I felt more than a slight twinge of disappointment at his rejection.

"You're a nice girl, Lucky. I'm not looking to get involved." His words came out harshly, and I was taken aback by the venom in them.

"Fine." I stared out of the window, visibly shaken and confused. Had I imagined the stares I thought we had shared? "I guess you have Angelique and all the other girls anyway."

"Angelique is a friend," he said smoothly. "She knows the score."

"She looked like more than a friend to me," I said jealously.

"She is more than a friend." His stare was challenging me to say something else, and I wanted to slap him.

"Okay," I said simply. "I don't really care."

"Lucky, you can't honestly tell me you're the type of girl who partakes in one-night stands?"

"No, I can't," I whispered, still upset. I should be happy that he hadn't tried to seduce me after everything I had been holding out for, especially now that I had met Braydon. Zane wasn't worth my time or energy. He didn't want me, and as far as I was concerned, I didn't want him either. I already knew he was a playboy.

We drove in silence, and I closed my eyes, hoping to get over the dull ache that reverberated in my heart. I wanted to shake myself for feeling down. I barely knew Zane, and what I did know wasn't exactly positive. He had none of the qualities I was looking for in a man. I couldn't afford to become emotionally attached to him. I needed someone who could provide me with what I wanted. Someone who would love me and be with me forever. Zane wasn't that guy. I knew that and had to accept it. I opened my eyes and saw a VW Beetle driving past, and I was just about to shout out "Punch buggy!" when I remembered I was in the car with Zane and not my parents. I bit my lip as I felt myself start to get emotional. It had been a long day, and a lot had happened, and I was starting to feel overwhelmed. I looked down at my phone, and all I wanted to do was call my mom. I just wanted to hear her voice telling me that everything was going to be okay and that boys came and went. I was glad when Zane pulled up into the driveway of what I assumed was his house. I jumped out of the car quickly, happy to be distracted from my thoughts.

"Wow, this place is huge," I said, impressed at the grandeur of his home. "Do you live here alone?"

"Yes." He nodded and walked to the front door. "Come on, let's go inside."

I followed him into the house, and it was all I could do to stop my jaw from dropping to the floor as I walked through the door. Zane's home was unlike anything I had ever seen before in my life. It was open plan, and I could see the living room, dining room, and kitchen, but the most amazing part was the view. The back of the house was made up of floor-to-ceiling windows and overlooked a huge pool and hot tub. The walls were painted white and had huge paintings on them. I was pretty sure I recognized a Chagall and my breath caught. There was a huge crystal chandelier hanging from the ceiling and I imagined my frat boyfriends trying to jump up and swing from it. I giggled to myself at the thought. This was the home of an educated and distinguished man, not some drunken Sigma Chi. The floor shone underneath my feet, and I realized it was solid marble. But it was the huge pool that beckoned to me from beyond the glass.

"I love your pool," I said shyly.

"Thanks, Noah used to swim in it every day. It was the reason we bought this place. It's Olympic size." He spoke matter-of-factly, and I turned to look at his face.

"Who's Noah?" I asked quietly, wondering if Zane was perhaps gay? Maybe that was why he wasn't really interested in kissing me, I thought.

"My brother." His voice was curt. "Let me show you to your room."

I followed him up the marble staircase quietly; it was obvious he didn't want me to ask him any more questions about his brother. I wondered where he was and why he had left this amazing house. I had a million different questions swirling around in my brain, but I kept them to myself. Zane didn't seem to be interested in my questions, and I didn't want him to think I was prying. I was, after all, almost like his staff. I felt slightly weird following him up the stairs as if I was his guest. I only really knew him from the diner. One encounter at a party didn't exactly make us fast friends.

"This is really nice," I gushed as I followed him into a huge room. I was starting to feel like a robot, but didn't really know what else to say.

"Let me go and get you some pajamas." His voice was rough, as he walked towards the door.

"That's okay." My voice was feeble. "I can sleep in my clothes." I spoke more loudly, wanting to show him that this situation wasn't making me uncomfortable.

He ignored me and continued walking to his room, and I sighed while running my fingers through my hair. I wanted to run into the bathroom and check my reflection in the mirror. I had a bad feeling that I looked like a mess, and I wasn't sure if I had smudged my eyeliner and mascara when I had been rubbing my eyes earlier.

"Here." Zane appeared in the doorway again. "You can wear this." He handed me a pair of boxer shorts and a soft blue T-shirt, and I looked up at him with a thankful glance.

"These look really comfortable." I smiled gratefully. "Thanks."

"No problem." He continued to stare at me and it looked as if he was debating whether or not to say something else. My heart started pounding as he gazed into my eyes, and I could feel my inhibitions going away. I had a feeling he was going to ask me to sleep with him. I also had a feeling that I wasn't going to say no. "Lucky, you can tell me to mind my own business, but why did you drive your car out late at night if you knew it had mechanical issues?"

"What?" I frowned in confusion. I had been preparing myself to accept his caress; I hadn't been expecting a lecture.

"I just don't think it's safe for you to be driving around late at night in a car that isn't very reliable." He frowned and leaned towards me. "I don't even want to imagine what might have happened to you if I hadn't been there."

"Why exactly were you there?" I shot back defensively. "It seems kind of suspicious to me that you were driving right behind me. I thought you had already left the party."

He looked away quickly and ran his hands through his hair and sighed. "I wanted to make sure you made it home safely."

"What?" I gasped. "You were following me?"

"I wasn't following you, per se." He shook his head. "And you should be thanking me. I saved your ass."

"My ass didn't need saving," my voice rose. "You are a creeper. I can't believe you were following me."

"I wanted to make sure you were okay, Lucky. You're too nice of a girl to be going to those types of parties."

"What's that supposed to mean?"

"The girls at those parties know the deal. They fit the lifestyle." Zane paused. "I didn't want to see you getting hurt."

"So what deal is that, Zane?" I frowned. "Do you mean these girls are all a part of 'The loose legs for Zane club'?"

"The what?" He looked at me and laughed. "Did you just make that up?"

"You know what I mean." I glared at him. "It seems to me that you seem to think you're the only one who can look after himself." I went off on a tangent. "I may be a girl, but I don't need you to come save me, Zane. You can save that for the two-dollar whores you take out every Friday night."

"That's a low blow, Lucky." He frowned. "And I'll have you know, I don't sleep with every girl I take out."

"Oh, really? So you didn't sleep with any of the girls I've seen you with at Lou's?"

"Well, hold on." He grinned. "I never said that."

My heart fell at his words. I was hoping he was going to say that he had never slept with any of them. That he was looking for Miss Right, and that was why he had gone on so many dates. In my heart of hearts, I had pictured him telling me that he had also been saving himself for his future wife. Then I would tell him that I had been saving myself as well, and we would ride off into the sunset together.

"So you've slept with most of them?" I looked up at him curiously, the causal expression on my face hiding the urgency behind the question.

"I'd rather not talk about my sex life with you, Lucky." He peered at me with a serious expression. "I'm sorry that you were uncomfortable with me following you, but I thought it was for the best. And it turns out, I was right. I followed my gut, Lucky, and my gut was telling me to make sure you got home okay."

"What about Angelique?" I bit out angrily. I was mad that he didn't want to tell me more about his dating life.

"She got home fine, I'm sure." He sighed and turned around. "I'm going to let you get some sleep. In the morning, we can call a tow truck and have it towed to the shop."

"I don't have any money to pay a mechanic yet," I sighed softly. "Well, I have some money, but not enough." I looked down at the lush cream Berber carpet beneath my feet, feeling embarrassed.

"We'll figure something out." He reached over and grabbed my arm. "I promise, Lucky. It'll be okay." His blue eyes crinkled warmly, and as he reassured me, they seemed to be trying to communicate to me in some unknown language. I felt myself trying to understand his silent message.

"I hope so." I sighed, letting my long brown hair cover my face. I was starting to feel even more confused, and I could feel a slight melancholy build up in me. A wave of exhaustion hit me, and I yawned loudly.

"Point taken, Lucky." Zane grinned and winked. "I'll see you in the morning."

"Night." I watched him as he walked out of the room and quickly shouted, "And thanks."

"No problem." He didn't look back as he sauntered down the hallway, and I quickly closed the door before pulling off my clothes and putting on his boxers and T-shirt. I sniffed the T-shirt to see if I could smell his scent, but it smelled like fabric softener. I laughed at myself for my cheesiness before getting into the king-sized bed. I moaned out in pleasure as I slipped in between the sheets. They reminded of hotel sheets, and I knew that they had to be 500-thread count Egyptian cotton. I moved my legs back and forth, loving the luxurious softness against my skin. I lay back with my head against the down feather pillows, and I wondered what Zane was doing and thinking. I felt a warm thrill in my stomach as I thought about him being concerned for me. It had been a little creepy that he had waited for me, but part of me felt exhilarated and cared for. He had to like me, at least a little bit, if he had been worried about me getting home safely. Unless he just saw me as an innocent, guileless local girl and he felt a responsibility for me because he saw me every Friday at Lou's. I felt disappointed then. Maybe he didn't really care for me at all. At least not in the way that I wanted.

I felt my eyes drooping and I yawned. I rolled over, exasperated with myself for continuing to hope that I meant something more to him. *He doesn't even know you,* Lucky, I thought to myself as I drifted to sleep.

***

I awoke about two hours later, sweating and delirious. I felt disoriented in the big bed and jumped out and walked around the room. I wanted to go home. I wanted to be in my own space and look at the photos of my parents. I wiped my face and cleared my dry throat and decided to go down to the kitchen to get a glass of water. I knew that I couldn't go back to bed right away. Not with the images of my parents so fresh in my mind. I walked lightly, hoping not to make any noise, as I looked around the house in awe. It was beautiful and large in a non-ostentatious way. This must be what Scarlett O'Hara must have felt every day at Tara, I thought as I floated down the stairs, imagining myself to be the lady of the manor. What would it feel like to live in a palatial home like this? I looked at the statues in the foyer, lit up by the moonlight shining through the window. I was a bit surprised at the décor of the house. It seemed to be a bit sophisticated for someone Zane's age, but what did

I really know? I jumped from the staircase to the ground, and the marble floor beneath my feet was cold enough to make me cry out slightly. I paused and looked up the staircase to make sure I hadn't disturbed Zane.

I walked quickly through the hallway and into the kitchen, trying to be as quiet as possible. I walked into the kitchen and looked around in amazement—it was beautiful. I was just about to open the doublewide stainless steel fridge when I felt something on my back.

"Argh!" I screamed and turned around quickly, my heart beating rapidly.

"Hey, sorry." Zane's voice was calm and slow, and he looked at me with a twinkle in his eyes. "I didn't mean to scare you."

"I was just coming to get some water," I muttered, unable to stop myself from looking at his naked chest. Zane looked even more handsome and muscular than I had imagined, and I was slightly overwhelmed by the urge to run my hands across his chest. "I was feeling sexy—I mean, thirsty," I quickly corrected myself, blushing furiously.

"I don't see why you can't have been feeling both ways." He laughed and opened a cabinet. "I think I'll join you in a glass."

"Did I wake you up?" I watched his biceps flex as he took the glasses out, and I swallowed hard.

"No, I couldn't sleep."

"Oh." I wanted to ask him why, but I didn't want him to think I was being nosey.

"I was about to go in the hot tub."

"Oh." I looked down and realized he was wearing a pair of swimming trunks. I stared at his muscular thighs and wondered if he played soccer. I had always had a thing for guys who played soccer.

"You're welcome to join me if you'd like."

"I don't have a swimsuit." *Please don't tell me you have one for me to borrow*, I thought to myself. I couldn't stand the thought of wearing one of his skanky girlfriend's outfits.

"We can skinny-dip." He winked, and laughed at my mortified expression. "I'm joking, Lucky."

"I knew that." I swallowed the water quickly, trying to ignore the telltale feelings in my stomach. "I should just go to bed."

"Or we can just talk?" He smiled. "If that would help."

"You don't want to talk."

"How little you trust me, Lucky." He cocked his head and smiled. "But actually, yes, I would love to talk."

I bit my lip and giggled. "I didn't mean that you wanted anything else or anything, just that maybe you wanted to relax and not feel the need to entertain me."

"Thanks for clarifying that." He grinned and opened a cupboard. "Want some cookies?"

"What cookies do you have?" I paused. "And do you have hot chocolate as well?"

"You're not going to eat cookies and drink hot chocolate as well?" Zane looked at me with a shocked expression.

"There's a reason I'm not a size zero." I laughed, suddenly feeling lightness between us. I wasn't sure what had changed between us. It was almost imperceptible, but I could sense a change in the way Zane was smiling at me.

"Will you make us both a hot chocolate if I can find the ingredients?" Zane pulled out a jar of Cadbury's drinking chocolate, and I opened the fridge to look for some milk.

"Of course."

"Will you dunk your legs into the hot tub at least?" He smiled at me. "As we drink our hot chocolate."

"I guess I could do that." I laughed.

"Okay, I have Lorna Doone shortbread and Oreos. Which one do you want?"

"Both." I laughed and grabbed an Oreo. "My parents used to call me the real cookie monster."

"Oh, yeah?" He made a face. "I used to be called Tickle Me Elmo."

"Really? Why?"

"Because I love to tickle." He reached under my arms and started tickling me. I shrieked and pulled away from him.

"Oh, stop." I laughed hysterically. "I'm too ticklish."

"Beg me to stop." He looked down at me, and I realized that he had me backed up to the counter. I felt his bare chest pushing against me, and I couldn't stop my body from reverberating into his as he tickled me.

"Zane, please." I gulped as I stared into his devilish blue eyes.

"Beg me," he purred down at me silkily.

"I'm begging you, Zane." I put my hand on his forearm and we stood still for a few moments, just gazing into each other's eyes.

"You have pretty hair," he said distractedly.

"Thank you."

"How old are you, Lucky?"

"I'm twenty-two." I licked my lips nervously and studied the cleft in his chin. "What about you?"

" Twenty-five." He stared into my eyes, unblinking.

"So many more playboy years ahead for you then, huh?" I heard the words coming out of my lips, and I wasn't sure why I had said them.

"You could say that." His eyes crinkled, and he stepped back from me. I wanted to groan because my body missed the warmth of his so close to mine but instead, I turned around to spoon out some sugar into the cups. "So you don't have a boyfriend, huh?" I heard his voice whisper into my ear, and I nearly jumped out of my skin at how close he was. I could feel his chest against my back, and his breath was tickling my ear.

"No, not right now."

"That's a pity."

"It is?"

"Yeah, a beautiful girl like you needs a man to …"

"I don't need a man for anything." I frowned, annoyed at his words.

"You obviously need a man to take care of you." He laughed and grabbed a cookie. "That's not a bad thing."

"I don't need anyone to take care of me," my voice rose, and I could feel my blood pressure rising.

"Every girl I know needs a man."

"I'm not every girl you know." I narrowed my eyes and pushed past him. "I think I'm going to skip the cookies and go to bed."

"Wait, Lucky." He grabbed my shoulder and sighed. "I didn't mean to upset you."

"I'm sure." I rolled my eyes at him, and I paused as I saw his eyes crinkle and look away from me.

"You're not like other girls, are you, Lucky?"

"No, I'm not."

"Shall we go and talk in the hot tub?"

"No, thanks." I twirled around. "I think I want to go to bed now."

"You think I'm a jerk, huh?"

"I think you are an egotistical ass, yes," I spat out, my harsh words belying the calmness in my face.

"That's heavy." He frowned.

"You date a different girl every week and tell me I need a man. I think anyone would agree with me. You are an ass."

"I don't date a different girl every week. Just because I take a girl out for dinner, doesn't mean it's a date."

"I don't even care," I sighed. "I have other things to worry about."

"I told you, I will help you with your car."

"I don't need your help."

"I need your help, though." His voice was low. "Can we go and talk please?"

I looked at him suspiciously. What help could he possibly need from me?

"Can't it wait?" I yawned, all excitement and adrenaline having left my body.

"It can wait." He smiled at me sweetly and stretched. I watched as his muscles flexed and I found my eyes on his sexy chest again. He had a light spattering of hair across his pecs, and I wanted to reach over and caress it. I wanted my fingers to confirm that his hair was as silky soft as it looked. I wanted to feel his arms around me, holding me close. I wanted my head pressed against his chest, listening to his heartbeat. Zane Beaumont was the guy I had been fantasizing about for months, and now here he was in front of me in all his glory. I held in a groan. I was mad at myself for wanting to be with this man in all the wrong ways.

"I'm going to bed." I turned around and ran up the stairs quickly.

"I don't bite, Lucky," he shouted up at me from the bottom of the stairs with a laugh, and I ran quickly to my room.

I jumped into the bed and stared at the ceiling, breathing heavily. All I could picture was Zane's face. I sighed and rolled over and tried to think about something else, but I couldn't get him out of my mind. As I drifted to sleep, images of Zane on top of me and kissing me all over flooded my mind.

CHAPTER FOUR

"LUCKY, ARE YOU AWAKE?"

"No," I groaned from the bed with my eyes still closed.

"Can I come in?" Zane's voice sounded too sexy for this hour of the day. "No," I groaned and rolled over.

I heard the door creak slightly as it opened and Zane walked up to my bed. "Good morning, Lucky."

"Not really." I rolled over and peeked at him from under the covers. I was slightly disappointed when I saw him wearing a grey T-shirt, and tried to ignore the urge to reach up and pull him down to me.

"Sorry for waking you up, but I figured we should go and get your car before it gets towed by the police."

"Oh, shit." I jumped up out of bed quickly. "I didn't think about that." I stumbled slightly as I hit the ground and Zane grabbed me around the waist.

"Careful. We can't afford to have you hurting yourself as well."

"I'm fine." I pulled away from him reluctantly.

"Good." He ran his hand through his hair, and I watched as he rubbed the stubble around his mouth. "So, I have a proposition for you."

"Oh, yeah?" I looked at him in surprise, wondering what he was going to say.

"I think it's something that will work for both of us. You need money, and I—" he continued, with a silky voice.

"I'm not going to be your paid escort," I blurted out. "I may need the money, but I don't need it that bad."

"Lucky, I was just going—"

"I know you think I'm a mess and that I need a man. But I don't. I can look after myself. I don't need your money, and I don't need you in my bed."

"Who said anything about bed?" He smirked.

"I don't want to be your sub."

"My sub?" He frowned. "Like my sandwich?"

"No," I whispered slowly. "I'm not a sexual deviant."

"And I am?" His eyes twinkled. "Lucky, how did you know I was going to ask you to be my sub in exchange for paying for your car repairs?"

"Wait, what?" I frowned up at him and groaned. "Sorry, just ignore everything I just said. I think I'm still half asleep."

"Were you dreaming about being my sub?"

"No, of course not."

"So just normal sex then."

"Yeah," I muttered and flushed. "I mean no. I wasn't dreaming about you at all. I don't even believe in casual sex. Well, not anymore."

"Oh?" Zane sat down on the bed and grinned at me.

"I need to go and shower." I turned away, flustered. "You made me confused waking me up out of my sleep like that."

"Don't you want to hear my idea first?"

"What idea?" I frowned, looking back at him.

"Sit." He patted the spot next to him on the bed. "Sit, take a deep breath, and listen."

I sat on the bed next to him and looked at him curiously. "You're really bossy, you know that?"

"I know." He grinned. "I also know you're not the quiet, sweet girl you seemed to be at Lou's."

"Disappointed?" I laughed, self-consciously running my hand through my dark brown hair.

"Not at all." He turned towards me and reached over and rubbed something by my eye. "Sorry, you had some sleep in your eye."

"Thanks." I felt breathless as his finger traced down my cheek.

"You're beautiful." His words were slow, and he spoke as if in a trance. "You're really beautiful."

"Thanks." I bit my lip, unsure of how to answer him. "I'm not really sure what to say."

"Can I kiss you?" He leaned towards me, and I shook my head.

"No." I held my breath, hoping he would kiss me anyway.

"I love that." He shook his head and laughed as he pulled away from me.

"Sure you do."

"You've got a smart mouth, huh?"

"Are you going to tell me your idea before my car gets towed, Zane?" I tried to pretend that I wasn't completely and utterly dazzled by him. "I don't have all day."

"I'm looking for someone to be my part-time assistant." He paused. "And I like and trust you, and I know from seeing you at Lou's that you have a strong work ethic."

"You what?" I looked at him like he was crazy. That was the last thing I had expected to hear. "You want me to work for you?"

"I know that's not as exciting as being my sub, but I need a girl Friday, so to speak, and you need money, so I thought perhaps we could make something work."

"I don't know." I frowned. "Between school and the diner, I don't have much time."

"Then I guess I'll have to find someone else." He jumped up off of the bed and walked towards the door, pausing and looking back at me just before he walked out. "Do you have any other suggestions for your car?"

"I, wait, what?" I jumped up and shook my head. "I didn't say no, I just said I don't know."

"Lucky." He frowned at me. "I don't have time to mess around."

"What?" I walked towards him. "You have barely even given me a second to think about this."

He sighed and looked away from me. "Maybe this wasn't a good idea. Maybe you wouldn't be such a—"

"I accept the position." My voice was firm and loud. I was angry at how dismissive he was being. "I accept the position, and I would like us to go and get my car now."

"Okay." He grinned. "Meet me downstairs in five minutes."

"Wait, aren't we going to discuss this further?"

"We can talk later." He exited the room and called back, "Downstairs in five minutes."

I rushed to the en suite bathroom and quickly washed my face. I wasn't sure what I had just accepted, but I felt really excited. Excited and scared at the same time. Zane Beaumont was not the sort of guy I should be getting involved with more deeply. I knew it in my soul, but something was drawing me closer and closer to him.

"I'm going downstairs now, Lucky." I heard Zane's voice, and I quickly rushed back into the room and pulled on my clothes.

"I'm coming." I ran down the stairs puffing, and I saw Zane laughing at me as I joined him in the foyer.

"You could have been a few minutes late." He laughed and grabbed his car keys, and I scowled at him. "Most girls are."

"I'm not most girls." I followed him out the front door and ran my fingers through my hair to get the knots out. I got into the passenger side of the car, and Zane pulled out of the driveway wordlessly. "So what's the plan?" I asked impatiently.

"The plan?" He looked at me sideways and raised his eyebrows.

"What am I going to be doing as your assistant?"

"Catering to my every whim." He smirked and whipped out his phone. "Hey, Gus, I'm towing a friend's car to your garage. Work on it, fix it, and bill me, okay?"

I looked at him wide-eyed as he spoke to someone on the phone and I frowned. How dare he just take control over what was going to happen to my car!

"I'm not sure what happened, but it broke down last night. Yeah, on the highway. She's lucky I was there." He hung up, and I leaned over to him.

"You didn't even ask if I wanted my car towed to your friend's."

"He's not my friend. He's my mechanic, and he's one of the best in Miami. It seemed to me you didn't have anywhere else you wanted it to go."

"That's not the point." I sighed. "You can't just make a decision like that for me. I already have a quote. I have no idea how much this guy is going to charge."

"Let me worry about that."

"I don't want to let you worry about that, if that's okay with you," I said sarcastically.

"Do you have something against men, Lucky?"

"Do you have something against women?" I shook my head. "You're insufferable, Zane Beaumont."

"I think I'm being a pretty nice guy." He shot a grin at me, and I turned away from him. I heard his phone ringing and rolled my eyes as I heard his voice purr into the phone.

"Morning, dearie."

I felt jealous as he spoke into the phone and quickly took out my phone to see if I had any messages. I felt a warm thrill shoot through me as I saw I had a text from Braydon, asking if I had gotten home okay. I texted him back quickly, trying to ignore Zane sweet-talking some girl on the phone.

"Maybe we can go for dinner?" he purred. "I'm not available for lunch today."

"Don't decline because of me," I hissed towards him, and I saw him frown as he pulled up behind my car, still talking into the phone.

"Angelique, can I call you back later?" He stopped the car, and I jumped out, not wanting to hear him sweet-talk the leggy blonde I had met the night before. "Lucky, get back in the car." Zane got out of his car and shouted at me as I walked to my car. "It's too dangerous for you to be standing on the side of the road."

"Can I check my car, please?" I huffed. "You are not my dad, Zane. Stop bossing me around."

"We are on a highway, Lucky. Stop being a baby and get in the car!" he shouted at me and grabbed my arm.

"Ow, that hurts," I squealed as he dragged me back to his car. "I want to check my car."

"It's the same as it was yesterday, Lucky," he grunted as he opened the door. "Sit down."

"Or what?"

"You don't want to know what."

"You're a real asshole." I scowled at him and crouched back as he leaned in towards me.

"Lucky, you are the most …" His voice drifted off as he kissed me, and I closed my eyes as his lips crushed down on mine. I allowed him to push his tongue into my mouth for a few seconds before I pulled away from him.

"What are you doing?" I asked breathlessly.

"Shutting you up." He grinned and slammed the door shut as I was about to shout at him. I sat back and watched as he pulled out his phone. Within a few seconds, I saw a tow truck pull up in front of my car, and I watched as Zane walked up to greet the tow truck guy. I sat in the car for a little bit, hoping to catch my breath before I got out of the car. I touched my lips softly, wondering at the tingle I still felt in them. I had never been kissed like that before: hard, passionately, and all taking. I was angry and lightheaded at Zane's touch, and as I got out of the car, I realized I had feelings for Zane. Feelings which made me think that accepting a position working for him would be a bad idea.

I walked up to the tow truck guy and ignored Zane's glare. "Hi, I'm Lucky Morgan, the owner of the car."

"Uh, hello, Ms. Morgan." The tow-truck driver looked at me curiously as I gave him my hand. "I'll have this over to the mechanic within thirty minutes."

"Thank you."

"Lucky, didn't I tell you to stay in the car?" Zane's voice was low and angry.

"I think my head gasket is gone," I continued talking to the tow truck guy. "You can let the mechanic know."

"Yes, ma'am." The man looked at Zane and then me, and walked back to his truck quickly.

"How dare you talk to me like that," I hissed at Zane.

"Lucky—"

"Don't you Lucky me." I pointed at him. "You can't treat me like one of your floozies."

"Will you please stop dissing the girls I date?" Zane looked at me with a frown. "Jealousy is not a becoming trait."

"I'm not jealous of anyone."

"I don't want you to be confused, Lucky." Zane grabbed my hands. "I'm sorry. I shouldn't have kissed you."

"I'm not confused. You kiss a lot of girls, I'm sure."

"I ..." he paused and looked away. "I'm not looking for a relationship."

"I figured that much."

"But I like you. I hope we can be friends." He squeezed my hand, and I felt my eyes grow heavy.

"Sure."

"Let's go to breakfast and we can discuss the job."

"I think Braydon wants to take me to breakfast or an early lunch." I suddenly remembered.

"Braydon Eagle?" He frowned.

"Yes."

"Tell him no." We walked back to his car, and he opened my door for me. I got into the car and pulled out my phone.

"I don't think so." I pretended to dial some numbers.

"Lucky. Do not go on a date with Braydon Eagle."

"Why not?"

"He's not the guy for you."

"Why not? Is he a player like you?"

"Lucky." He put his finger under my chin and stared at me hard. "Don't test my patience."

"Or what?" I rolled my eyes as he got into the car next to me, and I put my phone in my bag again.

"Can you just trust me here, Lucky?"

"Why? I don't even know you."

"You know me." His eyes bore into me, and I sighed. He was right. I knew that at the end of the day, he was a nice guy. He had always been a nice guy to me at the restaurant; what he did with the other women had nothing to do with me.

"Fine, let's go to breakfast." I let out a huge sigh and shook my head at him. "I don't understand you, Zane Beaumont."

"Sometimes I don't understand myself either." His tone was tinged with irony and another emotion I couldn't place. "But thank you for giving me a chance." His hand reached over to my knee and he squeezed it, looking at me gratefully.

"I don't know why," I whispered under my breath. I stared out the window, wondering what I was doing. I felt like I was Alice and was now in Wonderland. Everything I felt was upside down, and a part of my brain was telling me to just forget my rules and let this path take me wherever it wanted to go.

"I didn't wait all night for you to stop dancing around the room with Braydon like a contestant on *Dancing with the Stars* for nothing," Zane muttered.

I gasped. "Wait? You were waiting to make sure I didn't go home with Braydon last night, weren't you?" I looked over at him, glaring at his causal demeanor.

"I told you. I wanted to make sure you got home okay," Zane growled, and looked at me quickly. "You don't need to be hanging out with Braydon Eagle, Lucky."

"Because you're so much better, right?" I barked out at him and sat back, scared as Zane pulled over to the side of the highway, stopped, and turned towards me.

"I have to tell you something, Lucky."

CHAPTER FIVE

"WHAT YOU HAVE TO TELL ME HAS to be said on the side of the road and not in a restaurant?" I asked sarcastically.

"Will you just let me talk?"

"I suppose that's my duty, so go ahead." I bowed my head submissively with my hands clasped in my lap and waited for him to talk.

"Lucky, you're too much. You know that, right?"

"I'm waiting."

"Let's go and get breakfast, and I will tell you after we eat."

"Are you kidding me right now, Zane Beaumont? You're not just going to leave me hanging, are you?"

"I need a tall, black coffee before I can deal with you, Lucky." He laughed, and started the car and pulled back onto the road.

"I need pancakes and bacon." I licked my lips and laughed at his words. Why was it was easy to forgive Zane and his comments?

"I don't like my subs eating bacon." Zane's voice was light, and I laughed at his words.

"You're never going to let me off for that comment, are you?"

"Well, it's not every day that a girl asks me if I want her to be my sub." He paused for a moment. "And you know that I have to ask why you even asked me that now."

"Argh," I groaned, embarrassed.

"Is there something I should know about you, Lucky? Are you a student and server by day and a dominatrix by night?"

"Um, if I was a dominatrix, I wouldn't be asking you if you wanted me to be your sub." I laughed.

"So you know a lot about that world, huh?" Zane looked at me quickly with a slight grin, and I punched his shoulder.

"Actually, no." I laughed. "I've read a few books that were about couples who were living those lifestyles."

"And it made you interested?"

"No." My voice was sharper than I had intended. "No. I don't think I would be cut out to be a dom or a sub."

"Yeah, I don't think so either."

"What does that mean?"

"Just that I can't see you in either role in the bedroom."

"You've thought about me in the bedroom?" I gasped out, surprised and slightly tickled.

"Well, no." He laughed. "Let's change the subject. I don't want to get myself in trouble again."

"Uh huh." I knew I was taking the conversation down a slippery path, but I felt a flush run through me as I thought about him thinking about me. It was a warm and happy feeling, and I wanted to hold on to it as long as possible.

"I think you're addicted to sex."

"What?" I laughed.

"You're always bringing it up."

"No, I'm not." I rolled my eyes.

"Yes, you are."

"Then let's make a bet now. The next person to bring up sex has to give the other person—"

"A naked massage," Zane interrupted as he pulled into a parking lot.

"You wish." I rolled my eyes.

"Maybe I do." He licked his lips, and we got out of the car.

"Starting from now, the next person who mentions sex has to give the other person one hundred bucks."

"Whoa, Lucky, I don't want to take your money."

"I'll be taking yours and I'm not worried about taking it." We both laughed and walked into the IHOP.

"Oh, Lucky, so honest and confident."

"I'm thinking about what I'm going to spend my hundred dollars on," I purred, as we walked to our table. I opened the menu eagerly, trying to decide what I wanted to eat. My stomach was growling at the smell of grease, and I wanted to stuff my face with many items on the menu.

"Do you know what you want to get?"

"I want eggs, bacon, sausage, pancakes, toast, and hash browns." I laughed. "And I'm also eyeing the crepes."

"Small appetite."

"Well, you know how we supermodels do it."

"Oh, of course, you need a big breakfast before the catwalk."

"Exactly, or the wind will blow us away."

"We can't have the wind blowing you away now." Zane winked at me, and I leaned towards him with a grin.

"Exactly, not when I'm doing a service to mankind, showing off ugly dresses that cost thousands of dollars."

"If you want me to buy you one such dress, let me know."

"I can afford to buy it myself ..." I laughed. "Goodwill has plenty of designs that match those on the catwalk, and I can buy several outfits for twenty bucks."

"Well then, here you go." Zane took out his wallet and dropped twenty-dollar bill on the table. "Go crazy on me."

I grabbed the twenty and used it to fan myself. "Why thank you, Mr. Beaumont, I do declare I think you are my hero right now." I spoke in a deep Southern accent, and he laughed.

"Maybe I should introduce you to my dad, it seems to me you could have a huge career in acting."

"Why, whatever do you mean, kind sir? I'm no actress; I'm just a Southern belle."

"I do like me a Southern belle."

At this point, Zane and I were staring into each other's eyes, and our faces were inches away from each other. If I moved forward slightly, our lips would be touching.

"Hi, thanks for coming to IHOP. Can I get you guys some drinks?" A sour-looking older lady was standing at the table glaring at us, and I sat back quickly, embarrassed to have been caught in a non-intimate intimate moment.

"Can I have a small orange juice and a cup of coffee, please?" I smiled at the lady, and she stared back at me with a surly look.

"And you, sir?" She turned away from me and looked at Zane.

"I'll have the same thing as my fine young debutante."

The lady rolled her eyes and flipped a page on her notepad. "Are you guys ready to order or do you need a few minutes?"

"I'm ready. You, Lucky?" Zane wiggled his eyebrows at me, and I held in a laugh.

"Yes. I'm ready. I'll have the International Passport Breakfast, please."

"And I'll have a ham, green pepper, and cheese omelet, please." Zane smiled at the lady, and she gave him a hard stare.

"I'll have the drinks out in a few minutes." She turned around and walked back to the kitchen.

"And this why I come to your diner every Friday." Zane laughed.

"Oh, really? Why?"

"Because I have the best server in all of Miami at Lou's."

"Shayla is pretty good."

"Not as good as a girl named Lucky."

"Well, you know what they say. Girls who go through cotillion make the best servers."

"I guess I learn something new every day." He laughed and then frowned as his phone rang. "Sorry, will you excuse me please, Lucky? I have to take this."

"Sure." I smiled at him, trying to ignore the curiosity that was creeping up in me. Who was on the phone? I wanted to know, and yet I didn't. I knew that if I found out it was Angelique, my mood would be ruined. I decided to distract myself from eavesdropping on his conversation and pulled out my phone while I waited.

"Did you speak to him?" Zane hissed into the phone. "So what did he say?"

I bit my lip, wondering who had made him so angry.

"Flying?" He sighed. "Do you know who the girl was?"

I opened my text messages, pleasantly surprised to see that Braydon had texted me back, asking me to join him for dinner that evening. I was about to turn my phone off without answering when I heard Zane say, "I'll give her a call and see if I can take her on a date next week."

I kept my face down, hurt and upset, and quickly responded to Braydon's text: *That sounds great. What time were you thinking?*

"Sorry about that." Zane's voice interrupted me.

"No problem."

"So what were we talking about?" he asked me with a brief smile. His eyes looked distracted, and I could tell his mind was still on his phone call.

"I don't remember. Maybe you can tell me what you had to say?"

"What I had to say?" He looked at me with a blank expression.

"When you pulled over on the highway." I frowned. "You said you had something to tell me."

"Oh, yes." He paused. "It's not important."

"You can't just say that now. I want to know."

"Lucky." He leaned towards me again and spoke in a low tone. "I want you to be my undercover lover. I want us to reenact all the scenes from *Fifty Shades of Christian*, and ..."

My mouth dropped open as I looked at him. I knew he was a freak. Or more accurately, a kinky freak. "You what? Do you mean *Fifty Shades of Grey*?"

Zane burst out laughing and nodded his head. "Sorry, I had to see your face.   I take it you read the book?"

"That is not funny." I frowned and ignored his question. "You owe me a hundred."

Zane pulled out his wallet and took out another set of twenties. "In all seriousness, Lucky, I want you to come with me to Los Angeles tomorrow."

"I can't go to Los Angeles." I shook my head. "I have school, and I have to work."

"Okay." He sat back and smiled at the waitress as she placed our plates on the table.

"What do you mean, okay?" I frowned. "That's it. You're not even going to tell me why?"

"You told me you couldn't come."

"But that doesn't mean I can't be convinced." I sprinkled some salt and pepper across my eggs. "Convince me."

"What are you studying, Lucky?" Zane cut into his omelet. "Last night I think you told me history, right? You know a lot about civil rights stuff?" He spoke nonchalantly.

"Yeah, history." I nodded.

"I like history." He smiled as he chewed. "It suits you."

"Why does it suit me? Became I'm old and dowdy?"

"I'd hardly call a supermodel old and dowdy."

"Then why does history suit me?" I couldn't stop myself from laughing.

"It shows me that you're a thinker. You're intelligent. You care about the past, about people, and about not making the same mistake twice."

"What did you study in school?"

"I was a British Literature major." He grinned. "A very useful degree."

"About as useful as it is to know the names of all of King Henry VIII's wives." I laughed.

"We all know about King Henry VIII." Zane laughed. "He left the Catholic church so he could get a divorce from Anne Boleyn, right? Or was it Catherine of Aragon?"

"Smart." I stuck my tongue out at him. "Name for me all of his wives, and I'll be even more impressed."

"Do they have to be in order?"

"No." I grinned.

"Okay, that's easy." He grinned back at me. "Catherine of Aragon, Mary, Anne Boleyn, and um, the other Boleyn sister."

I burst out laughing as he frowned. "The other Boleyn sister?"

"Right?" He cocked his head. "Or was that a movie?"

"I guess knowing all his wives' names isn't that common, right?"

"Okay, you got me. What are the names?"

"First off, *The Other Boleyn Girl* was a book by Philippa Gregory. Now his wives, in order were:

Catherine of Aragon, whom he divorced; Anne Boleyn, whom he executed; Jane Seymour, who died; Anne of Cleves, whom he divorced; Kathryn Howard; who was executed, and another Katherine, Katherine Parr."

"What happened to the last Katherine? Did she run away, scared he was going to scream 'Off with her head!' or what?" Zane faked a shudder.

"Actually, no. Henry died while they were still married and she was widowed."

"I bet she poisoned him." He laughed.

"Well, that would have been karma for sure." I laughed and cut into my crepes. "Mmm, these are so good." I allowed the taste of the lingonberries to dwell in my mouth as I chewed slowly, savoring every bite.

"Come with me to Los Angeles, Lucky." His voice was low and measured as he changed the subject.

"I still don't know why you want me to come."

"I need an assistant. Preferably someone who knows a lot about history. I need someone I know I can work with and trust. And I trust you. I don't trust many people."

"But I have classes," I sighed.

"Can you take a leave of absence or withdraw from the classes?" He paused. "I'll pay for the classes you've already signed up for so you're not out any money, and I will pay for the remaining credits for any other classes you have to take."

"I don't know." I bit my lip. "I'm almost done."

"I'm working on a documentary." He paused. "It's about the sixties. Civil Rights and all that stuff. I think that you could really help me, as a historian."

"You make movies?" I looked up, surprised and slightly bewildered. Why hadn't he told me before that he was making a documentary about the Civil Rights Movement?

"Well, not movies. Documentaries." He smiled. "My dad makes blockbusters; I just dabble, so to speak."

"What's your documentary about?"

"The education system after 1954."

"You mean after *Brown v. Board of Education*?" I asked excitedly.

"Yes. I'm talking to people to see how the end of segregation impacted their educational experiences."

"Nothing really changed that much." I paused. "Not for a long time."

"You know about the subject?"

"A bit." I drank some coffee and thought for a moment. "My senior thesis is related to that topic, actually."

"Oh?" He nodded his head and smiled. "Well, then it seems like you would be a better assistant than I thought."

"I'm not sure."

"You could be one of the interviewers if you want. Maybe use what you learn to help your research. Talk about an amazing primary source."

I nodded in agreement. It would be an amazing opportunity to actually talk to people who were alive and went through integration, as opposed to just writing about interviews that other historians had been a part of and written about. This was the sort of research that could get me into a top graduate program, which would offer me a better chance at a tenure-track professorship at a top university.

"I'd have to stay in school for an extra semester, though." I talked out loud, voicing my concerns.

"What's an extra semester compared to the time of your life? Think about it, Lucky, you have your whole life to live as everyone else has planned for you. Do you know what that six months means to the breadth of your life? It means nothing. This could be a real growing experience. Opportunities like this don't just come up for everyone. This is an opportunity to break up the mundane everyday-ness of your life."

"I just have a plan, you know?" I frowned to myself. My plan had always been to graduate in four years, get married, go to grad school, have some kids, and become a teacher or professor. But where had it actually gotten me? It was like my boyfriend plan. Good in theory but going nowhere. I was practically a nun right now, and there was no potential guy anywhere on the horizon. Well, maybe on the horizon, if things went well with Braydon. "And I'm kind of seeing someone right now. I don't just want to leave."

"I thought you didn't have a boyfriend." Zane's voice was accusing.

"I don't, but I have a first date tonight."

"With?"

"That's none of your business."

"Are you going to come with me to Los Angeles?" He sat back, and I watched as he wiped his mouth with his napkin.

"I …"

"Take a chance, Lucky. I promise you won't regret it."

"I don't even know you."

"Do you want me to talk to your parents? I can call them now and talk to them if you're worried about what they're going to say."

"I'm not worried." I looked away from him and stared at a little boy who was blowing bubbles into his chocolate milk at the next table.

"This is an amazing opportunity, Lucky, I'm sure they would understand." I felt Zane's hand reach over and grasp mine, and I turned back to him.

"My parents don't have to understand. They're dead."

I saw the sympathy in his eyes as soon as I said the words and I cringed. I didn't want him to feel sorry for me. I didn't want every conversation we had from here on out to center around his pity for me. "And you don't have to treat me any differently because of that, either."

"I won't treat you differently."

"Good."

"Let me take you to dinner tonight."

"I have a date." I frowned. "I told you that already."

"So I'll just pick you up tomorrow morning then?"

I nodded slowly. "I guess so."

And that was it. My decision was made. I think I had known as soon as he had asked what my answer was going to be. "I have to call Shayla and Maria at the diner to let them know," I shook my head as I spoke. "I can't believe I'm doing this."

"You won't regret it, Lucky. I promise." Zane's eyes looked slightly overwhelmed as he smiled at me. I didn't really understand why. All of a sudden I wondered if I had made a mistake. How could I just give up college and my job? All for a guy I didn't really know and a job I hadn't even started yet. I bit my lip and sighed. All my walls were crumbling down and I wasn't sure what was going to happen next.

CHAPTER SIX

"YOU LOOK AMAZING, LUCKY." BRAYDON whistled as I got into his car. I was slightly annoyed that he hadn't come to my door to escort me but tried to dismiss those feelings from my head.

"Thanks."

"Do you like my car?" He grinned as he stretched his hands out and caressed his leather seats.

"It's a nice car." I nodded, slightly uncomfortable at the way he was stroking the seats.

"It's a Bugatti," he continued. "Nice doesn't even begin to describe it."

"Oh, sorry." I had no idea what a Bugatti was.

"Don't be sorry, just sit back and enjoy the smoothest ride you'll ever feel."

"Uh, okay." I attempted a smile, but I was pretty sure it came out as a frown instead. Braydon laughed as he looked at my face, and I felt even worse.

"I'm sorry, Lucky. I'm a bit over-the-top about cars. I guess it's a guy thing."

"That's okay." I smiled, genuinely this time. "I'm just not one to know much about cars." I laughed slightly at my comment. "Well, other cars, at least. I know a bit about mine."

"Oh, what do you drive?" He looked at me curiously.

"A Toyota Corolla. 1991." I laughed at his pleasantly bored expression. "And right now, it's in the shop, inoperable, so I'm not really driving anything."

"Oh, that sucks." He pulled out into the street. "Well, let's go get some dinner. I figured I would take you to the Rusty Pelican in Key Biscayne. That way we can look out on the water."

"That sounds great." I smiled and looked out the window, feeling a little tense. Why hadn't he asked me about my car—or how I had gotten home last night? It seemed like he didn't even care. Not like Zane did. I frowned as Zane popped into my head. There was no point in my comparing Braydon to Zane because I knew that Zane didn't want a relationship, so there was no point in my thinking about him in that way. I had to ignore the feelings his kiss had ignited in me, feelings that had been there from the first time I saw him. If I was honest with myself, I had been attracted to Zane from the first moment I saw him, but I also knew that he was the sort of guy I should avoid. Nothing positive was going to come from a relationship with Zane—if I could even call it a relationship, since the most he would want would be to be friends with benefits. That I was sure of. And I didn't want that. It didn't fit in with my Last Boyfriend Plan at all.

"Earth to Lucky." Braydon's voice interrupted my daydreams and I turned to him with an apologetic glance.

"Sorry, I was just thinking."

"Why, isn't that a novel thing to do?" He laughed. "Most girls I know in Hollywood chatter inanely about their makeup and clothes."

"But I'm sure you still want to date them." I laughed.

"Well, you know." He grinned at me. "That was the old me. The new me is ready for a girl of substance."

"Oh, yeah?" I studied his boyish face and smiled at him warmly. "You know, I feel really weird driving in a car with *the* Braydon Eagle."

"You shouldn't."

"It's not every day that an everyday girl like me goes to dinner with a Hollywood movie star like you."

"Well, then, we should get some champagne at dinner to celebrate an extraordinary day."

"This is an extraordinary day." I nodded in agreement, thinking more about the agreement with Zane than my date with Braydon.

"I like your honesty, Lucky." Braydon laughed. "I'm not sure I've ever met a girl like you before."

"I'm not sure I'm this exotic breed that everyone keeps saying I am." I laughed self-consciously.

"You are all that and more." Braydon pointed to a high-rise as we drove. "I live over there."

"Oh, yeah?" I peered out the window, but didn't see anything other than a bunch of tall buildings.

"You ever come to Brickell?"

"Not really."

"It's boring." He laughed. "I'd much rather live on the beach."

"So you can party all day and night?"

"Something like that. Though my manager wouldn't like it if I did."

"Probably not," I agreed.

"So, Lucky, tell me the name of your favorite movie."

"Of all time?"

"Of all time! Oh, and it can't be one of mine." He laughed. "Just in case you felt obligated to name one of mine."

"Well, you know ..." I giggled. "I think my favorite movie is *My Fair Lady*."

"Oh." He paused. "The rain in Spain—"

"—is mainly on the plain," I finished for him. "I love Audrey Hepburn. She was such a classic actress."

"Yes, she was. It's funny that you chose *My Fair Lady* because her co-star, Rex Harrison, is my favorite actor."

"Oh, yeah?"

"Yes, I love Alfred Hitchcock movies and I thought he was superb in *Midnight Lace*."

"Oh I've never heard of that movie."

"It's not Hitchcock's most famous piece of work, but I loved it. Doris Day is in it as well."

"I'm not sure who Doris Day is, I'm afraid." I looked at him apologetically.

"You don't know Doris Day?" His voice was aghast. "Maybe we should skip the restaurant and just go and watch movies." He laughed.

"That could be a plan." I smiled.

"Doris Day was probably the greatest actress of her time. She starred in tons of movies with Cary Grant and Rock Hudson."

"Ooh, okay." I still had no clue who she was.

"Okay, she sang that song about whatever will be will be, you know the one, 'Que Sera, Sera.'"

"Oh, yes. I love her." My voice was loud with excitement. "I had forgotten her name. My mom used to watch her movies all the time."

"Okay, phew." He laughed. "So you like *My Fair Lady* then, huh?"

I nodded, my head filled with happy memories. "I don't know why, but I always watch it when I'm down. It's my go-to movie."

"I see." He stopped the car and I looked at him in surprise. "We're here."

"Oh, wow, that was fast." I looked out the window and saw the yacht club. "I've never been here before."

"It's a pretty cool place. I'm not sure why they call it the Rusty Pelican, though, there's nothing rusty about it. We'll get a table outside and stare out onto the water."

"And the bright lights." I grinned.

"Well, of course, if there were no bright lights, we'd be sitting there scared that a gator might come out of the water and attack us."

"I certainly don't want to be attacked by an alligator."

"Me either. Have you seen my face?" Braydon grinned and I laughed.

"I sure hope you're hungry," he continued, happy I was laughing at his jokes.

"Oh, I am." I nodded my head. I hadn't eaten since breakfast.

Zane had dropped me off after we had eaten and he had been slightly peeved that I hadn't told him who my date was with. I was annoyed and upset when I got to my room because Zane had been so dismissive when I had gotten out of the car. I didn't understand him. His moods seemed to go back and forth so quickly. I sighed. I was supposed to call him when I got home so he could tell me what time he would be picking me up to leave the next day. Everything was going so quickly that I barely had time to think about everything. I was starting to feel overwhelmed, and had spent the afternoon in bed watching TV instead of packing.

"Lucky, are you home?" Once again, Braydon interrupted my thoughts of Zane.

"Sorry. I have a lot on my mind."

"I can see that. I hope it's not another guy."

"Oh no, of course not." I blushed and turned away.

"I like your dress, by the way." Braydon looked me over and smiled. "It's very chic."

"Um, thanks." I smiled gratefully and tried to hold in a laugh. I had gotten the dress from Target for $24.99, and I was pretty sure Braydon was the only one who had used that adjective to describe the dress.

"Let's go eat." He grabbed my hand and I followed him through the restaurant and then through a door.

"Wow." I stepped out the door and saw the candlelit tables overlooking the great expanse of water that was lit up by the huge condos on the other side. "This is magnificent."

"I had to make our first date special." Braydon smiled and we sat down. "And let me recommend the Strawberry Mule to drink, it's delicious."

"Done." I grinned. "Alcohol and strawberries sound good to me."

"I love a girl who is easy to please."

"Well, that's me." I laughed.

"On our next date, I'm going to take you on my boat."

"Oh." I bit my lip and leaned forward. "About that …"

"Oh no, did I do something wrong already?" He sighed and slapped his forehead.

"No, no, no. Not at all," I was quick to reassure him. I was actually enjoying my time with Braydon. More than I thought I would. "I'm having a good time, but I'm actually leaving Miami tomorrow."

"Wait, what?" He frowned. "For good? Aren't you in school?"

"I am in school." I smiled, slightly embarrassed. "I'm going to withdraw from my classes and I'm not sure how long I'll be gone."

"Sorry. I'm really confused here."

"I got a job. It's related to my major, so I thought it would help me in my career, you know."

"Are you going to be teaching history to kids in Africa or something?"

"No." I laughed. "I'm going to be helping with a documentary that will be focusing on the era of my studies."

"Oh, wow. A documentary?" He looked intrigued and then the expression on his face changed and he looked somewhat angry. "Please do not tell me that Zane Beaumont is in any way involved with this documentary."

I bit my lip and stared at Braydon's handsome face across the table. I didn't know what to say.

"He is, isn't he? That asshole."

"He's not an asshole," I spoke quietly, defending a man I wasn't sure actually deserved to be defended.

"He did this because of me, you know," Braydon hissed. "He must have heard me telling Evan how nice I thought you were and how I was interested in you."

"I'm sure he didn't hire me because of that." I frowned.

"Trust me." Braydon frowned. "I didn't even know he was making a documentary."

"Well, he is." I looked down at the menu, uncomfortable with where the conversation was going.

"He needs to just get over this bullshit," Braydon swore and I saw his fists clenching.

"What bullshit?" I asked curiously.

"With Noah." He frowned and looked out at the bay. "He needs to fucking move on."

I sat back and wished that I was still at home. Braydon's mood had changed and I was no longer comfortable in his presence. "What does Noah do?" I asked, hoping to finally get some information about Zane's brother.

Braydon looked back at me with clouded eyes, and attempted a smile. "Let's not talk about the Beaumonts right now."

"Okay." I tried to hide my disappointment. What was the big secret about Noah?

"So where in L.A. will you be?"

"I'm not sure." I shrugged.

"Can I come out and see you?"

"Come out where?"

"To L.A., silly."

"Oh. Sure. Though, I'm not really sure how busy I'll be."

"Can I ask you something, Lucky?" Braydon's voice was serious and I nodded slowly, wondering what he wanted to ask me. "Do you like me?"

"I think you seem like a nice guy, yes," I answered, truthfully.

"Could you see yourself dating me?"

"I don't know." I frowned. "I don't really know you well enough to answer that."

"Would you give me the opportunity to get to know you better?" Braydon looked bashful. "I'm not sure I've ever met a girl that Zane and I both seem to like."

"Sorry, what?" Why had he brought up Zane's name?

"It's obvious to me that Zane wants to get into your pants. I don't know if he was interested in you before he saw us together, but I'm pretty sure he wants you now. I don't—"

"Stop." I held my hand up. "I like you, Braydon. You seem like a nice guy. Please don't bring Zane into this. I would like to get to know you better. If you're in Los Angeles, give me a call and we can talk."

"I don't want you to get hurt, Lucky. Zane's not a nice guy," Braydon said earnestly.

"And you are?" I laughed, not quite believing that both guys had warned me off of each other.

"I am, actually." He sat back. "I have a good family. My parents are still together. I'm looking for love. Real love. Not Hollywood love."

"I see."

"I'm sure plenty of guys say that though, right?"

"Some do."

"I don't expect you to trust me just because. I would like to prove myself to you."

"You don't even know me." I looked at him incredulously. "I'm no one. You don't have to prove anything to me."

"I'm going to sound crazy right now, but have you ever just met someone and knew?"

"Knew what?"

"Knew that they were the one?"

"I don't know." I bit my lip. "I think that's lust."

"Lust is immediately knowing you want to get into bed with someone." He laughed. "I've felt that many times, but that's not what I felt when I saw you for the first time."

"Oh?"

"You looked so innocent at the party. You stood out among all the other girls. I saw you cringe when Evan started talking to you. I saw the red creep up your face, and I saw the look of thanks as I came to save you."

"Thank you for that, I wasn't sure how I was going to get away from Evan." I faked a shudder, hoping he would change the subject.

"And as soon as you looked into my eyes, I felt a connection with you." Braydon chuckled again. "I feel like I'm in a movie right now. This has never happened to me before."

"It does feel like a movie, doesn't it?"

"I'm going to be honest, Lucky, I've haven't been the best guy. I've done things I'm not proud of, but I'm serious about wanting to settle down."

"This isn't a proposal, is it?" My voice rose with fear. I knew I sounded crazy, but I had read enough celebrity magazines to know that actors moved fast when they wanted to. Braydon seemed like a nice guy and I wanted a guy who was looking for a serious commitment, but I wasn't a desperado.

"A proposal?" Braydon looked taken aback and I laughed.

"Okay, no need to have a heart attack. I was just checking. You never know with you guys."

"I'm coming on pretty strong, huh?"

"You could say that." I sipped my drink. "Let's just enjoy some good food. I think I've had too many intense conversations today."

"Okay. That sounds like a plan." Braydon looked bashful and I felt bad for him, but I was not in the mood for another life-defining moment.

"I guess it would be too much to ask you what other intense conversations you had today?"

"Yes, yes it would." I racked my brain for something else to talk about. "So what made you want to be an actor?"

"My parents." He laughed. "My mom was obsessed with Hollywood. She had tried to be an actress for so long, but she never made it, so she ended up marrying my dad instead. And from the age of six months, she paraded me to every agent there was. I suppose it helped that I was a cute kid."

"With your thick blond hair and big brown eyes." I laughed.

"Yeah." He grinned. "I got lucky, actually." He laughed. "No pun intended. The blond-haired, blue-eyed babies were a dime a dozen, but the blond-haired and brown-eyed kids were pretty hard to come by."

"You were a diamond in a store of sapphires." I groaned at my analogy. "Well, you know what I mean."

"Yes, I do. And you're correct. I was lucky and got cast from an early age, and there's been no looking back."

"Now you're Braydon Eagle, successful movie star." I smiled gently, still slightly fazed that I was sitting across the table from him. I felt a bit troubled that I wasn't able to enjoy the moment more, as my mind was still on Zane.

"Well, if you think riches equal success, then yes. But if you equate success by good friends and love, then no." He sighed.

"Well, you have one, and hopefully, the others will come soon."

"I hope so as well." He looked at me intently. "It's funny. They say that one man can't have everything. But I want to prove them wrong."

"You mean the career and money versus love debate?"

"Yeah. I used to think for a long time that love was closed off to me. Being an actor, you never really know who you can trust. I thought I would just have to accept the groupies and accept that I would have a trophy wife. But now …"

I didn't want to ask him, *but now what?* In all honesty, he was starting to get on my nerves. He had only known me for a day or so. I'm not a bombshell and I didn't think my conversation had been that witty, either. I mean, I know I'm pretty friendly, but I didn't think I was great enough to warrant the endless stream of wonder and praise that was emanating from his mouth. Perhaps his real goal should be to move from acting and become a poet. He certainly knew how to wax on. I started laughing to myself at my wax on thought and Braydon looked at me curiously.

"Sorry, I didn't mean to be funny. Am I boring you?"

"No, of course not." *Yes, you are boring me,* I thought. "Let's talk about something else. This isn't a Hollywood movie. We don't have to fall in love in five seconds and have two point four kids in as many years."

"I've been accused of being a bit too serious in relationships."

"Oh?" Relationships? What was he talking about? I kept a pleasant smile on my face, but I was starting to think that Braydon Eagle was bonkers, and perhaps on drugs as well. I giggled and kept my head down. *Shit,* I thought to myself. The alcohol was getting to me. I was a pretty light drinker and I was pretty sure that this drink contained a high level of alcohol. I could feel that I was a little tipsy and I was scared I was going to tell Braydon just how ridiculous he was acting. And I didn't want to do that. There was something about Braydon that I liked deep inside. He seemed like an honest, genuine guy. And I was surprised that I wasn't in awe of him.

"What are you thinking right now, Lucky?"

"I'm thinking that this is a totally cool moment." I grinned. "I'm here sitting with a huge star and I feel like I'm out with a regular friend."

"I like that." Braydon smiled and we both laughed as a woman ran up to the table and asked him for an autograph. As Braydon smiled at the young lady and signed her napkin, I wondered at how down to earth he seemed. He was the sort of guy that I felt could make me happy. He was a forever sort of guy. I sat back and smiled to myself. Maybe everything was going to work out after all.

***

"I'm so sorry for getting you home so late." Braydon parked his car and turned to me. "I didn't think we would be out this long."

"It's okay." I hiccupped and closed my eyes. "I shouldn't have had so much to drink."

"You only had three." He laughed.

"I'm pretty sure each drink was like two and a half normal drinks," I sighed. "I only hope I don't have to be up too early tomorrow morning."

"What time is Zane picking you up?"

"I forgot." I started to shake my head and groaned. "Oh, my gosh. I need to go to bed. I feel like I'm going to be sick."

"Oh, no." Braydon jumped out of the car and ran to open my door. "Maybe you should get out?"

"I don't want to puke in your Fiat," I agreed.

"It's a Bugatti."

"Huh?" I frowned. "But it looks like a Fiat because it's flat." I laughed. "You have a flat Fiat and a big, hairy cat and it's sitting on the mat wearing a woolly cap, no, no, wearing a woolly hat. The cat in the hat on the mat in the Fiat." I laughed and fell against Braydon as he helped me out of the car.

"You're really drunk, aren't you?"

"Nope." I hiccupped again. "I'm just relaxing before Zane takes me to L.A. to be his assistant."

"Yeah." Braydon frowned. "You don't have to go, you know. If you need a job, you can be my assistant."

"Really?" I looked at him in surprise. "Would I get a Fiat as well?"

"I don't …"

"Wait until I tell Shayla and Maria that I'm getting a Fiat." I laughed and then stopped still. "Oh, nooo, I can't remember if I called them and told them about my new job."

"I'm sure you can do that in the morning."

"I'm so bad."

"I'm sure they will understand." Braydon held on to my waist as we stood on the pavement. "Are you sure you don't want to work for me instead of Zane?"

"Zane brings a different girl to the diner every week. Can you believe that?" I shook my head. "A different beautiful girl every week. He is a player."

"That doesn't surprise me."

"I have no interest in him, you know that?" I shouted. "I do not want him to kiss me."

"Can I kiss you?" Braydon leaned in towards me and I stared up into his brown eyes.

"If it's a kiss you want, you may have it," I sang loudly and stuck my face up into the air with my eyes closed.

"What's going on here?" I heard Zane's deep, gruff voice and opened my eyes, feeling disoriented. Was I so drunk that I was now having hallucinations?

"Zane," Braydon sighed and stepped back from me. "What are you doing here?"

"I came to make sure Lucky got home safely," Zane growled at Braydon as he glared at him. "I've been trying to call her all night."

"Zane?" I peered at him. "Is that you?"

"Are you okay, Lucky?" He walked over to me and stared down into my eyes. I felt like he was trying to look into my soul.

"Is that you, Mr. Big Tipper?" I laughed and touched his arm. "Oh, you're real."

"Are you drunk?" He sighed and I bobbled.

"And I need to go to bed."

"I was just taking her inside." Braydon glared at Zane and attempted to push him out of the way.

"I think I've got it from here, Eagle." Zane grabbed my arm and turned his back to Braydon. "Lucky, are you always this reckless?"

"Huh?" I frowned at his angry tone.

"Last night you drove home late at night in a car you knew was faulty, and tonight you get drunk on a dinner date with a guy you barely know."

"I know him."

"You met Braydon before the party?"

"Well, no, but I know him from movies."

"Lucky," Zane's voice sounded really angry, and I cringed.

"Lucky, do you want me to escort you inside?" Braydon interjected.

"I'm okay." I shook my head and held on to Zane. "Thanks for a great evening. I'll see you soon."

"Yes. I will be in Los Angeles very soon." Braydon smiled sweetly at me. "And think about my offer as well. I would love to have you work for me."

"I will." Hiccup.

"Let's go." Before I could say a word, Zane was pulling my arm and dragging me away from Braydon.

"That hurts," I groaned.

"What job is Braydon talking about?"

"Huh?" I frowned and closed my eyes. "My head hurts. I just want to go to bed."

"Lucky, what if he'd tried to sleep with you?"

"Who?" I yawned, overcome with sleepiness.

"Braydon." He sighed.

"You smell good." I buried my head into his chest.

"Is this your door?"

"Yes." I smiled up at him.

"Where are your keys?"

"My keys?" I closed my eyes again and put my arms around his waist. "You are so warm."

"Lucky, your keys." Zane pulled me away from him and I groaned.

"They're in my purse," I pouted and then giggled as he took my handbag from me and took out my keys.

I stared at him as he opened the front door and I wondered at how handsome he was. He was too good-looking. "You're too hot, you know that?"

Zane ignored me and dragged me through the front door. "Okay, show me to your room." He closed the door quietly and looked at me seriously.

"Are you going to carry me?" I giggled.

"No." He frowned and sighed again. "What would you have done if I wasn't here, Lucky?"

"Nothing." I frowned back at him. "Why?"

"Do you know what Braydon could have done to you?" His voice was angry again. "Do I have to watch you 24/7?"

Something in his voice reminded me of something that had been in my brain since I had seen him. "Why are you here?"

"I told you. I was worried. I wanted to make sure you were okay." He led me up the stairs. "And don't try and change the subject."

"I'm not a baby. You don't need to check up on me."

"I've been calling you all night."

"Oh, my battery died. Stupid phone."

"It's irresponsible to go out with a dead phone battery," Zane growled. "Especially when going out with a guy like Braydon."

"All Hollywood guys aren't bad."

"I hope he didn't drug you," he hissed. "I've never seen you like this before."

"But you've never seen me out."

"I saw you last night."

"But I wasn't really drinking." I hiccupped. "I knew I had to drive home. I don't drink and drive."

"Well, that's good. I also advise that you don't drink when you go out on dates with shady guys."

"Why do you dislike Braydon, Zane?" I asked him seriously. "Wait, this is my room." I stopped suddenly.

"Okay, let's get you into bed."

"You want me in your bed like all the other girls, don't you?" I winked at him.

"No, I don't." Zane shook his head, and I felt a wash of disappointment run through me. Even now, when all my inhibitions were gone, Zane Beaumont didn't want me.

"I wouldn't sleep with you anyway."

"Oh, yeah?" He looked at me with a twinkle in his eyes. "Why's that?"

"'Cos Braydon likes me and he could be my last boyfriend."

"Your last boyfriend?" Zane looked confused.

"The guy I'm going to marry, duh." I fell onto the bed.

"You're going to marry Braydon?"

"I don't know." I yawned. "But it's a possibility. So that's why I can't sleep with you."

"Okay, that makes sense," he drawled. He stood there awkwardly next to the bed, and I grabbed his arm and pulled him down next to me.

"You are so handsome but you always look so serious." I stared at him. "But you are also so nice.

You're one of my favorite customers, you know. And you fixed my car. But you're a real asshole as well."

"You sum me up so perfectly." He grinned and pushed me over. "If I'm going to lie on your bed with you I need a bit more space."

"No fair. You made my head hurt," I groaned.

"Let me make it better." He kissed my forehead and brought me close to him. "How does that feel?"

"Hmm." I closed my eyes and pushed my head against his chest. "So nice and cool." I felt his arms around me and I snuggled into him. "You are so warm and yummy."

"Oh, Lucky," he sighed.

"Yes, Zane?" I purred against him.

"You're going to be the undoing of me," he whispered and held me tightly.

"I'm the best server you've ever had."

"Yes, you are." He laughed and I felt his hands rubbing my back as I drifted to sleep.

CHAPTER SEVEN

MY HEAD WAS KILLING ME WHEN I woke up. I tried to stretch, but my arms hit a solid wall. I opened my eyes slowly and yawned widely as I was still feeling tired.

"Oh," I exclaimed, as I awoke to Zane's gaze. He was staring directly into my eyes and he had a bemused expression on his face. "What are you doing here?"

"I think your first words should be 'thank you,'" he said with a deadpan expression.

"Thank you?" I frowned, trying to remember what had happened the night before. And then it all came crashing down. "Thank you? Are you joking? You frigging embarrassed me last night. Poor Braydon. What must he be thinking right now?"

"I hope he's thinking that he better not bother you anymore," Zane growled.

"What?" I squinted at him. "He better not be thinking that. I hope he doesn't think that we're hooking up," I groaned. "Man, you may have just ruined everything."

"Ruined what?" He made a weird expression. "You don't seriously think you're going to marry him? I thought that was the alcohol speaking."

"I never said I was going to marry him," I sighed. "I just said that, perhaps he could be my last boyfriend."

"You confuse me, Lucky." He sighed. I studied his face and wondered how he could look so handsome first thing in the morning.

"I confuse you? Is that a joke?"

"I don't understand you." He frowned and ran his hands through his hair.

"What's to understand?"

"Everything." He turned away from me and looked at my walls. "I like your room. You have nice style."

"You mean for a poor person?" I laughed, thinking about his lavishly furnished house.

"No, for any type of person." He pointed at some posters on my wall. "I love Monet."

"Me, too." I smiled. "I thought about studying Art History for a while."

"But you decided on British History?"

"British History?"

"You know so much about King Henry VIII."

"Oh, yes. I forgot about that conversation. I changed my focus from the reformation to the Civil Rights Era."

"Oh, yeah. My civil rights expert." He grinned. "You're one smart cookie."

"Not really, but I guess I am compared to the other girls you date." Oh no, why had I said date? We weren't dating. We weren't even friends. He was my boss now. And he was in my bed. I wanted to groan out loud. What was going on here?

"Well, you know. I have to change it up." I felt his arms around my waist and he pulled me towards him. "Let's see if you're a better kisser as well."

"Wait, what?" My eyes widened as I felt his hands on my ass. "Um, what's going on here?"

"I'm going to see if you're better than my other girls in every way."

"Zane," I spoke his name quietly, my lips were mere inches away from his, and I was aching to feel them on mine.

"Yes, Lucky?"

"Why were you waiting there for me last night?" I frowned. "It's kind of creepy, you know. Just waiting outside my house."

"Are you saying you think I'm a creep?"

"No." I paused. "Well, you know." I stared into his eyes, looking for some answers. I didn't understand

Zane Beaumont and I really needed to. My heart was thumping and my skin was tingling. My stomach was jumping at being so close to him, and all I wanted was to make love to him. Maybe it was because I was still slightly hung over. Or maybe it was because we were both lying down in my bed. All I knew was that I wanted to have sex with Zane Beaumont. It was almost inevitable. I had felt this way from the first moment I had met him. When I was with him, I forgot about my rules. About the plan to wait for one special guy. I just needed to be with him. To feel him. I wanted him. It was as simple as that. I was willing to deal with the heartache. What was one last heartache? I'd been through it before. I survived.

"Kiss me," I whispered. I didn't want to think any more. All I wanted was to feel his lips against mine. I wanted to feel his hands on my skin.

Zane grinned and leaned towards me. I felt his lips press against mine, hard and rough. His hands went behind my head and he brought me closer to him. I felt his tongue creep into my mouth, and I kissed him back hard. He tasted too sweet for the morning. I was enveloped in his taste and our tongues tangled together passionately. I gasped in his mouth as I felt his hand on my ass, pushing me into him. Our bodies were pressed together and I felt his manhood against me, aroused and shifting. I moved my body so I could feel him better and he chuckled, rolling me over onto my back, so that he was on top of me. His lips never left mine and he shifted himself in between my legs, his erection struggling against the confines of his pants. I wrapped my legs around his waist and pulled his body down, closer to mine. His chest crushed into mine and my breasts were delighted at the close contact. I wanted to feel his naked skin against mine and I pulled up his T-shirt, trying to pull it off.

Zane pulled away from me slightly and kissed down my chin to my neck. I felt his right hand creep up to caress my breast and I moaned as he squeezed it. All of my nerves were on edge and I wanted to feel his hands on my naked skin. I wriggled below him and finally got his shirt off. I ran my hands over his back, delighted by the feel of his skin. He was warm to the touch and he groaned as I rolled him onto his back and sat on him. I looked down at him panting and bent down to kiss his chest, running my hands across his nipples as I kissed down his happy trail.

"Oh, Lucky," he moaned and I felt his hands in my hair.

"Hmmm." I kissed back up his chest to his lips and started grinding on top of him. I smiled at the feel of his hardness beneath me and rocked back and forth as he kissed me. He wrapped his hands around my waist and dropped them to my ass until he was cupping my butt cheeks and pushing me down into him further. I reached down to his belt buckle, wanting to release his dragon, but Zane stopped me.

"No." Zane rolled me back over and lay next to me, kissing my nose. "I don't think this is a good idea."

"What?" I sighed and leaned over to him. "Why not?"

"You're not that type of girl."

"What type of girl?"

"The type of girl that has casual sex without getting feelings."

"What?" My cheeks flamed at his words.

"I'm not the guy for you, Lucky." His eyes looked bleak. "I'm not looking for a happily ever after. I never want to get married."

"You just want casual weekly sex?" I rolled away from him.

"No." He sighed. "But I also don't want a serious relationship."

"Who says that is what I want?"

"I knew from the very first time that I saw you at Lou's that you're not the type of girl for a casual anything." There was mirth in his voice. "Don't be mad at me, Lucky."

"I'm not mad." I jumped up. "It's ... whatever. I don't need you to have sex with me."

"It's not that I don't find you attractive, Lucky. You're hot." He sighed. "Shit. You just felt how much I want you."

"Whatever." I blushed.

"Wait." He jumped off the bed and pushed me against the wall. He then grabbed my hand and pulled it to his manhood. "You feel that?"

I nodded mutely, slightly angry, but totally turned on.

"I want to make love to you until you cry out my name, Lucky," he whispered in my ear as my hand closed in on him through his pants. "I want you to take me in your hands and in your mouth. I want to feel myself in you. I want to make you blush as you come for me."

My eyes widened at his words and then I felt his tongue in my ear and I felt even more turned on than I had been before. My hand dropped from his crotch and I ran my hands through his hair. I closed my eyes and reveled in the feelings he was awakening in my body. It had been too long since I had made love. I was feeling horny and my panties were starting to feel uncomfortable between my legs.

Zane pulled away from me and stared into my eyes. "You're a special girl, Lucky, but I'm not the guy for you. I'm not going to take anything from you that I shouldn't."

"I'm not a virgin," I whispered, wanting him to take me.

"Go and take a shower, Lucky." Zane sighed and backed away from me. "We have a lot to do today."

I looked at his face, embarrassment coloring mine. "Yeah. I need to let Maria and Shayla know I'm going to L.A. for a bit."

"Lucky, if you don't want to take this job, well, you can back out."

"Do you want me to back out?" I questioned, holding my breath.

"No." His eyes bore into me and I felt a secret thrill.

"So then I'm coming."

"Did you withdraw from your classes?"

"I'm going to do it online today." I tried to keep my breathing normalized. I was starting to feel slightly panicked. Didn't he want me to come anymore? I didn't want to think about how much that hurt me. I didn't want to acknowledge the fact that I was really starting to fall for him.

"Have you told your roommates?"

"Oh, I forgot." I slapped my hand against my mouth.

"Oh, Lucky." He smiled. "We can tell them when you come out of the shower."

"Oh." I bit my lip and stared at him. He looked so hot without his shirt on, but I knew I had to think about something else. "They're going to think you stayed the night."

"I did stay the night."

"But they're going to think we had sex." I mouthed the last part.

"Are you scared to say sex, Lucky?" He moved in closer to me and winked. "We did very nearly have sex. Is that so bad?"

"You don't understand." I sighed. "I haven't had sex in a while."

He looked surprised at my statement and I continued. "I've been saving myself for a guy who I think will be worth it." I flushed, hoping he didn't draw any conclusions about my feelings for him from my statement.

"So you haven't had sex in a while?" He smiled softly, and I blushed. "But you were going to have sex with me?"

"No." I turned around quickly. "I'm going in the shower."

"No … what?"

"Just drop it, Zane."

"I'll never understand you, Lucky." Zane shook his head and sighed. "You're the most complicated girl I've ever met."

"And that's saying a lot." I grinned and stuck my tongue out at him. He responded with a swift slap to my butt, and I ran out the door laughing, wondering, once again, what I was getting myself into.

CHAPTER EIGHT

"WOULD YOU LIKE SOMETHING TO DRINK, madam?" the flight attendant asked me with a huge smile.

"Some water, please." I smiled at her from the luxury of my first-class seat.

"And you, sir?"

"I'll have a rum and Coke, please."

I looked at Zane aghast. "You're drinking?"

"Why shouldn't I be?" He grinned at me and sat back.

"Weren't you the one telling me about alcohol just this morning?"

"I told you it's not smart to drink around shady guys."

"Here's your water, ma'am. Are you sure you don't want anything else?"

"I'll have a glass of champagne, please," I looked at her uncertainly. Did they even have champagne on planes?

"Of course."

"Alcohol?" Zane raised an eyebrow at me.

"I can hold my own around shady guys." I smiled sweetly and turned to look out the window. I heard him chuckle and grinned to myself. "So where am I going to stay in L.A. and how much am I going to be making?"

"I'm surprised you haven't asked before now." Zane shook his head. "You're way too trusting, Lucky."

"Are you telling me I shouldn't trust you?"

"I'm telling you that you shouldn't trust anyone else too easily."

"But trusting you is fine, right?"

"I'm looking after your best interests."

"Why?" I questioned him.

"I feel like we've developed a friendship these last few months."

"Really?" I laughed. "Was this before or after I presented you with your entrees?"

"It was somewhere between soup and salad."

"Aw, now I know why you always gave me big tips. You were making sure your friend made a good wage."

"Well, you know. That's what friends are for." He laughed. "But in all seriousness, you'll be staying with me at my condo."

"Oh, okay."

"I hope that's okay. I'll be able to make sure you stay out of trouble."

"I'm not a kid, Zane," I sighed. "I don't need another dad."

"You're my responsibility, Lucky. Humor me, it will make me feel better. Okay?"

"I guess. But I'll have you know, I'm twenty-two, not twelve."

"A twenty-two-year-old who makes bad mistakes."

I rolled my eyes and turned away from him. Zane obviously had some sort of protector complex. I doubted I would be able to talk him out of it. "Does Noah live there in the condo as well?"

"No." He frowned and put his earphones on.

Well, okay then, I thought to myself. I guess I still wasn't going to find out about Noah. I didn't understand what the big deal was, but I knew I didn't want to push the issue. I hoped Zane would tell me himself when he was ready. I put my earphones on and flicked through the channels. I couldn't quite believe that I was on a plane to Los Angeles. The day had seemed to fly by. After my shower, Zane and I had told my roommates that I was leaving and then we had dropped by Lou's Burger Joint. Shayla's and Maria's jaws had dropped when I walked in with Zane. I still didn't think they believed me when I had told them we weren't going on some sex-fuelled vacation. I laughed, thinking about Shayla's expression when I told her I was withdrawing from my classes and going to L.A. She had taken me to the side and told me that I could come back to Lou's whenever I wanted. I had given her a big hug while holding back a sob. Shayla was like my family. I was going to miss her and Mike a lot.

I felt Zane tap me on the shoulder and I turned to look at him with a questioning expression. "How did your parents die?" he asked me softly.

"I— what?"

"You don't have to talk about it if you don't want." He smiled at me gently. "My mother left my brother and me when we were young." He scratched his ear. "It's still hard to talk about."

"Your mother left you?" I pulled my earphones out and turned to him.

"Well, she left my father, she wanted to spite him. My brother and I were just the dregs at the bottom of the barrel."

"Oh, I'm sorry." I reached out to touch his hand. "That must have been tough."

"It made Noah and me closer." He paused. "We were young. I was six and Noah was four."

"Oh, wow." I felt tears welling up in my eyes at the thought of Zane being abandoned as a child.

"I still remember her." He stared into my eyes. "She had blonde hair that was almost white. You wouldn't know if you looked at me. But Noah, he had the same white-blonde hair. It made my father hate him even more. All because he reminded him of her. We both have her eyes."

"She must have been beautiful."

"She was." He avoided eye contact with me. "Too beautiful for my dad, really. She was young when she married him. Got caught up in the lifestyle."

"Did she marry him for money?" I asked softly.

"No." He laughed at my surprised expression. "You would have thought so, right? What woman leaves her husband and two young children if she loved them?"

"Why did she leave?"

"I don't really know." He paused and finished his drink. "My dad never said and she never contacted us."

"Do you know where she is now?"

"No." He shook his head. "Noah and I used to say that while the sun shines and the moon glows, we don't need anyone else in our lives."

"That's sad." I frowned. "And I don't think it's too healthy, either." I started to realize that his mother's abandonment must have been the biggest reason for his resistance to relationships. "Everyone isn't like your mom."

"Maybe not." He reached over and ran his hands over my hair. "But love, lust, whatever it is, it's not enough. All it does is lead to heartbreak."

"I don't believe that." I frowned, my heart aching for him. "Not all love leads to heartbreak."

"Didn't your parents' deaths break your heart?"

"Well, of course. But it wasn't their fault."

"But don't you get it?" He shook his head. "It doesn't have to be on purpose, it will still break your heart. Love will tear you apart from limb to limb."

"So you'd rather not love?"

"I weigh the odds. I'd rather have a fun and enjoyable life than to fall deeply in love with someone and have my heart pulled out of my body."

"You don't know if your heart will be pulled out of your body, as you so eloquently stated."

"I'm pretty sure love equals pain."

"My parents loved each other and me with all their hearts until the day they died. And every day I miss them with all my heart. I miss my mom making me spaghetti and meatballs when she sensed I had a bad day. I miss my dad taking me to the library every Saturday morning to choose five library books. I miss his goofy grin when I would choose a *Sweet Valley Twins* book. I miss going to Pizza Hut and ordering three personal pan pizzas, because none of us could agree on what toppings we wanted. I miss my dad grabbing my mom's hand and sneaking kisses when he thought I wasn't looking. I miss them being proud of me and loving me. And every single night, it hurts when I think of them. It hurts when I go to bed and I know I'm going to wake up the next morning and they still won't be around. It hurts every time I want to call them, or email them, or go home for the holidays. But I wouldn't give up one second of those memories to eradicate the pain that I feel every day. It hurts and it burns, but my love for them still lives on." I blinked away tears as I took a breath and I knew he could see the pain in my eyes.

"You're a strong woman." He took my hand in his. "I'm so sorry about your parents."

"And they died in a car crash, by the way." I sighed. "They were driving to Miami to see me. They wanted to surprise me for my birthday. I was surprised, all right."

"It wasn't your fault." Zane looked at me in concern.

"It was a semi truck." I wrinkled my nose. "The driver was texting and cut across the interstate. The police told me they died instantly. That gave me some peace of mind that they weren't in pain."

"How long ago was this?"

"About a year and two months ago." I bit my lip.

I had been devastated, unable to function. And when Justin had dumped me, I had felt like my world was caving in on me. I had thought that I would never escape the pain that consumed me and kept me in my bed for days. I had vowed that I would never again give myself to a man who didn't truly love me and want me. My heart, body, and soul are too precious to give away lightly. But at least I was still open for love, I thought to myself. I couldn't imagine what it would be like to be so crushed that love would never be an option in my life. I wouldn't want to imagine what amount of pain would make someone never want to feel love ever again. Or maybe the problem was that he had never really experienced love. Maybe he didn't know what he was missing.

"That was pretty recent." He paused. "I guess we've both been through the ringer and back."

"I guess so."

"You're a special girl, Lucky. I know I've told you that before, but I want you to understand how much I mean it. I've never really met anyone like you before."

"You don't really know me." I laughed, slightly delirious and uncomfortable at his words.

"I've watched you for months in the restaurant." He smiled. "You are always happy, always friendly. I've heard you talking with your coworkers, giving them advice, taking shifts. You've always been pleasant when you've seen me, even though I take a different girl in there every week."

"I understand why now."

"No, no you don't." He frowned. "But that's okay. You don't need to know."

"Okay." I pulled my hand away from him. I was hurt by his words. It seemed to be a one-way street with him. I was always open with my feelings and thoughts, but he always seemed to have something to hold back. I wanted him to tell me about Noah, I wanted him to open up about the things he tried so hard to keep inside. But I didn't want to force him. I wanted him to want to tell me those things. My heart hurt slightly as I sat there. I was falling for Zane Beaumont, and I knew there was no way we could ever have a happy ending.

"Lucky, I may not be Mr. Wonderful and I can't give you everything you deserve in a boyfriend, but I can be your friend. I want to be your friend." He took a deep breath and his eyes looked so serious that I felt my body tremble at the intensity of his words. "I think we have a special connection, you and I. And yes, I'm attracted like hell to you, and yes, I want to make sweet love to you, but it's more than that. I want to be here for you. I can't give you my heart and I don't want yours, but I want to be there for you. In as many ways as you will let me."

As he stopped talking, I felt my heartbeat racing faster and faster, as if it were trying out for a position on a Formula One racing team. I wasn't sure how to respond to him. One part of me wanted to reach over and kiss him and tell him that I never wanted to let him go, but another part of me was cognizant of the fact that he had clearly told me that I would never have his heart and that he didn't want me to fall in love with him either. There was no future in a relationship between the two of us. After everything I had been through, I didn't know if I could survive being in a relationship with Zane that would never go anywhere. *But he's never known love*, a little birdie whispered in my ear. *Maybe if you show him what it means to be in love, maybe then he'll change his mind.*

"Did I scare you, Lucky?" Zane looked at me with worry in his eyes, and I shook my head.

"No. I'm just thinking."

"Not about being my sub again? Do I have to buy a paddle to get an answer out of you?" he joked with twinkling eyes and I burst out laughing.

"You better not buy a paddle. I don't think my behind could take it."

"Just my hand, then?" He winked and I lightly slapped his arm.

"I'm not really sure what you're asking of me." I spoke lightly, unsure of myself.

"I don't really know either." He sighed. "I guess I just want to see what happens?"

"Won't it be weird? Me, working for you, living with you, and kind of seeing you?"

"Only if we let it be weird."

"I guess." I bit my lip. I wanted to ask him about the other girls, but I was scared. It wasn't like he was asking to be my boyfriend. But I had to know. "Will we be dating other people?"

"I can't answer that for you." He rubbed his face. "However, if you're sleeping in my bed, I will not stand for you to be fucking another man."

"Zane." I looked around the airplane, mortified that someone may have heard his crude language.

"I don't share," he spoke softer this time. "I want your body all to myself."

"So you think you're going to have my body?"

"Only if you want me to."

"Okay." I laughed at the look on Zane's face as he heard my response.

"Just okay? No yes or no?"

"I have to think about it." I smiled. "Now, can I watch my movie?"

"I suppose. Seeing as it's been a long day, you can watch your movie."

"Why, thank you, kind sir, I do appreciate it." I spoke in my Southern accent again.

"I'm glad you find it agreeable, ma'am." Zane laughed and leaned over and kissed me on the cheek. "A man, such as myself, likes a woman to be soft and pliant," he whispered in my ear, and before I could respond indignantly, he was kissing me. I kissed him back passionately and closed my eyes. I could get used to these moments, I thought.

CHAPTER NINE

"WELCOME TO LOS ANGELES." ZANE grinned at me as he pulled into a parking space.

"I can't believe you let me sleep the drive away. I didn't see a thing." I yawned as I stretched in my seat.

"You needed your beauty sleep."

"I guess so." I stepped out of the car and looked at the building in front of me. It looked like a grand Spanish house. "You said you live in a condo?"

"It doesn't look like a condo, does it?" He grinned.

"No. It doesn't."

"I decided to bring you to my casa in Los Feliz instead." He grabbed the bags and I followed him to the front door.

"Why?" I was puzzled at the change in destination.

"No reason." He opened the big wooden door and I followed him inside. I was immediately struck at how different the interior of this home was compared to his place in Miami. The floors were a golden brown hardwood that ran from the front door all the way to the French doors at the end of the large room. From the front of the house, I could see the garden outside, and it looked lush and green with different plants and flowers. The lights at the back coupled with the moonlight made his garden look magical.

"Welcome to my home." Zane put the bags down and ushered me in properly.

"Thanks." My voice was small as I took in my surroundings. I was in awe at just how perfect his home was. There was a large white couch to the immediate right of me with bright orange throw pillows that seemed to accent the cream and orange rug on the floor. There was a huge fireplace to the right of the rug, and on top of the mantelpiece there were little ornaments. There were paintings all along the walls, but I didn't recognize any of them from any of my art classes or trips to museums.

"Do you like?" Zane asked me quietly and I could sense that he was really interested in my opinion.

"I really love it, Zane," I gushed. "It's so different from your place in Miami."

"That's really Noah's place," he explained. "This is my house. I chose it and designed it. This is my style. I've never really brought anyone here before."

"Oh?"

"Yeah." He shuffled his feet nervously. "I usually take everyone to the condo I share with Noah. It's in Burbank."

"Oh, okay." I offered him a small smile, while inside, I was beaming. This had to mean something, right? He had taken me to his real home and not the home he has on show.

"Would you like a tour?" He seemed unsure, and that uncertainty endeared me to him even more. He was like a little boy showing off his favorite toy. My heart went out to him when I realized that he likely hadn't had a great childhood, and that his image of the world had been shaped by events that had occurred in his life when he was six.

"I would love a tour. What are we waiting for?" I linked my arm through his and smiled up at him enthusiastically.

"Well, this is my living room."

"Who did the paintings?"

"I'm involved with a hospital that does research on children with cancer. These are some of the children's paintings."

"Wow. They are amazing." I looked at the paintings and was blown away by the talent of the children and the fact that Zane had hung their images in frames on his walls.

"The ornaments on the mantle-frame are keepsakes I've gotten from my travels."

"Do you like to travel a lot?"

"I did." He paused. "My father used to take us all over the world with him when we were younger. He had a lot of movie releases in other countries."

"That must have been fun."

"It was a great way to learn about other cultures and people. Many of the guys I know, all they care about is their own small microcosm—it's all about movies or parties. There's more to the world than having a good time."

"I agree."

"But that's a conversation for another time. This is my dining room. I got the table, solid wood by the way, shipped from India." Zane pointed to the huge table as we continued walking through the house.

"It's gorgeous."

"The chairs aren't very comfortable, I'm afraid." He laughed. "I have to get them replaced."

"At least they're pretty to look at."

"Who knew metal chairs would be so uncomfortable?"

"Not me."

"And through here is the kitchen. Some people don't like white cabinetry, but I love it, I think it looks so fresh and clean. I got the hardware at Anthropologie."

"I didn't know guys knew about Anthropologie."

"Oh, I didn't. A girl I was dating at the time took me in one day and I ended up finding quite a few pieces that I liked."

"Oh, that's cool." I tried to ignore the knotting jealousy in my stomach. *What girl?* I thought to myself. Was she his girlfriend?

"And, of course, all stainless steel. And a gas oven."

"Do you cook a lot then?"

"No." He laughed again. "I've thought about getting a cook, though."

"I can cook for you if you want. I really enjoy cooking."

"That would be great. If you don't mind, of course."

"I wouldn't mind at all."

"Awesome. Well, let's go upstairs. Let me show you the bedrooms."

"Oh, we aren't going to go outside?" I pointed to the French doors.

"We can go later. Maybe we can even go for a swim."

"You have a pool here?" I said excitedly.

"Of course." He grabbed my hand and we ran up the stairs. It was really light and spacious with a lot of windows. I was pleased to see carpet on the floors. I like hardwood a lot, but there is something about having carpet in the bedrooms that makes you feel more comfortable and at home.

"Let's go to my room first." He winked and I followed him to a door at the end of the hallway. I walked in slowly and looked around carefully to see what I could figure out about him from his room. I was surprised that he had a queen-sized bed in the center of his room, and directly opposite from it there was a 42-inch flat screen TV hanging on the wall. His nightstand contained only a lamp and a book, and his duvet was a shiny navy blue color that I hated. I looked to the corner of the room and saw a huge bay window. Next to the window was a small bookshelf with timeworn books that looked well read and there was a huge chest of drawers against the wall. I walked over to the bookshelf to see what books he had, and was pleasantly surprised to see the names of authors I loved and enjoyed as well.

"What's your favorite book?" I asked him curiously.

"My favorite? That's hard." He paused. "But my top three would have to be *Crime and Punishment* by Dostoevsky, *For Whom The Bell Tolls* by Hemingway, and *Paradise Lost* by Milton."

"Nice choices."

"What about you?"

"Well, I have to admit, I have a bit of an eclectic taste." I laughed. "I love *A Tale of Two Cities* by Dickens, I preferred *The Brothers Karamazov* by Dostoevsky, and of course my absolute all-time favorite is *Little Women* by Alcott."

"Classics." He grinned.

"Yeah, but I also love books like *Beautiful Disaster* by Jamie McGuire, and as you know, I've read *Fifty Shades*, and I enjoyed it."

"Well, that's because you were training to be a dom." He laughed. "Or should I say a sub."

"I think you should say nothing." I laughed.

"I'm afraid I don't have any secret pleasure or pain rooms."

"Wait, how did you know about the red room of pain?" I asked suspiciously. "Did you read it as well?"

"Hell, no." He laughed and shook his head. "Well, not really. I saw part of the movie script."

"Oh." I coughed. "Sure, that was it."

"Are you calling me a liar?" he growled and walked towards me.

"No."

"Yes, you are." He grabbed me and tickled me under my arms until I was squealing and almost falling to the ground. "Come here, you." Zane pulled me towards him and put his arms around me. He leaned down and kissed my forehead, and then my nose and my lips. I melted against him and we stumbled back onto his bed as we kissed. Zane pulled away from me slightly. "Are you ready to go to bed?" He studied my face and I knew he was asking me a completely different question.

"You haven't shown me my room yet." I looked away from him quickly, unsure of how to answer his unspoken question.

"Come on, then." He jumped off of the bed quickly and I followed him quietly. I had forgotten how easily he moved on from everything. I was annoyed at him and myself for not pushing the issue. "I figured you could have the room next door." He spoke in a perfunctory voice, all teasing gone from his tone.

"It looks very nice. Thank you." I looked inside the room and was once again overwhelmed by just how much the room fit my taste. The walls were a light yellow and the carpet was plush beneath my feet. I was happy to see the bedspread was a luxurious-looking cream color and the pillowcases were peach. There was a bay window in this room as well, and there was a vanity table and stool on the other side of the room.

This design had definitely been planned with a female in mind. I wanted to ask him why this room was so feminine; what had been his plan when he had created this room?

"I'll go downstairs and get your bags so you can get ready for bed," he said coldly.

"Oh, ok, thanks." I sat on the bed as he walked out of the room and I sighed. "Are we going to be working tomorrow?" I asked him when he returned with my suitcase.

"No." He shook his head. "I thought I would show you around Los Angeles this week and we could talk about the project. We will start officially working next Monday."

"Okay, that sounds good." I smiled, trying to break down his wall.

"I thought we could have a party in the next two weeks? Just a small one with some of my friends. That way I can introduce you to some people."

"That would be great." *Will Noah be there?* I wanted to ask him but resisted.

"I think I'm going to go shower. Feel free to help yourself to anything you want in the kitchen. You have a private bathroom through that door."

"Are you going to bed?" I bit my lip, not wanting the day to be done already.

"No, I was thinking of watching a movie after my shower." He frowned. "And after I make a few calls."

"Can I watch the movie with you?" I asked hesitantly.

"Sure." He paused. "If you don't mind watching it in my room."

"That's no problem." I smiled up at him happily.

"Okay. Good." He smiled back at me and rubbed his forehead. "I'm glad you're here, Lucky."

"Thanks. I'm glad as well." I watched him walk out the door and I lay back on the bed as he closed the door. I closed my eyes and took a big deep breath. The room smelled of tangerines and honey. I took another deep breath and stretched on the bed. I opened my eyes and looked around at the room again. It was beautiful and I was happy to be here. I jumped up and opened my suitcase, trying to decide what to change into after the shower. I wanted to make sure I looked cute and sexy, but not wanton. I didn't want him to know that I was going out of my way to look attractive to him. I was disappointed that he hadn't tried harder to keep me in his room. I wanted him to seduce me. I wanted him to want me so badly that he couldn't keep his hands off of me. Sometimes I felt as if that was how he felt, but other times, I felt as if he couldn't be bothered at all. I decided to wear a pair of gym shorts and a tank top—relaxed, casual, and slightly sexy, if Leeza was to be believed. I was just about to go into the bathroom when my phone rang.

"Hello."

"Hey, Lucky, it's Braydon. I just wanted to make sure you made it to the best coast all right?"

"Ha ha, I did make it to the west coast just fine, thanks."

"I'm glad Zane wasn't a completely ass to you then."

"Oh. No, he was fine." I paused. "Sorry about last night."

"What's to be sorry about? You had a few drinks. You were fine. Zane, on the other hand, was a psycho stalker."

"He was just worried about me."

"Why? He barely knows you," Braydon scoffed.

"Well, he knew my car broke down, and I guess—"

"Your car broke down?"

"Oh, yeah, I didn't tell you? I thought I told you on our date?"

"I think you said something about your car. But you're only now telling me he just happened to be there when your car broke down."

"Well, it was after the party, and I guess he left around the same time," I said defensively.

"Lucky, I want you to be careful." Braydon's voice was low. "I know you don't really know me. But please be careful with Zane. He's not right in the head, and I think he has something against me."

"What?" I was starting to get annoyed at Braydon.

"I know this may be hard to believe, but I think he has it out for me. Maybe he's jealous or something. But he is really not right in the head."

"Braydon, why would you say that?"

"Look, I don't know him that well. We don't really hang in the same circles. But his brother Noah and I were pretty tight. I think—"

"Hey, where is Noah now?" I interrupted him, hoping to get some information on the infamous Noah Beaumont.

"Zane hasn't told you?" Braydon's voice was slow and deliberate.

"No, and I haven't wanted to intrude. Did they have a falling out or something?"

Braydon sighed and took a deep breath. "Look, I don't want to say much, but Noah and Zane fell out. And Noah kind of left Zane behind. He wanted to make something of himself. He wanted to be a new person. Zane is so insular. He was all about it being him and Noah against the world, but Noah wanted more than that."

"Oh, wow, so they did have a falling out."

"Yeah." Braydon cleared his throat. "Look, Lucky, I want you to stay safe, okay? I'm going to try and fly down to L.A. this week."

"Wait, where is Noah now?"

"I gotta go. I'll talk to you later." And with that, Braydon hung up and I was no closer to knowing where Noah was. I sat looking at my phone and wondered what could have come between Zane and his brother. It seemed like they were as tight as two brothers could have been. Maybe Zane didn't like Braydon because Noah stole his friendship. Someone who was as emotionally insecure as Zane probably found it pretty hard to trust anyone. All of a sudden, I realized that I wanted to fix Zane. I wanted to be the one to let him see that not all relationships ended badly, that not all love was selfish and hurtful. Even if it cost me my heart. Zane was like no other man I had met before. On the surface, he seemed cocky, bossy, and uncaring, but I was starting to get to know the real him, and he was a really good guy. The sort of guy who could win my heart forever. He was the type of guy a girl took a chance on, and that was exactly what I was going to do.

CHAPTER TEN

"HEY, CAN I COME IN?" I KNOCKED on the door and opened it slightly so I could be sure Zane knew I was there.

"Hey, come in." Zane was lying on top of his bed in a pair of black gym shorts and another grey T-shirt. His hair was still damp from his shower and he looked cleanly shaved.

"Thanks. Are you still on for a movie?"

"Am I ever." He ushered me into the room and slapped the empty space next to him on the bed. "Have a seat."

"Thanks." I climbed onto the bed next to him, feeling slightly self-conscious.

"Do you like your room?" Zane leaned against the headboard and stared at me.

"It's really nice. Really feminine," I answered, hoping he would provide some insight to the room.

"I'm glad you like it." He nodded and smiled. I held my breath as he looked me up and down slowly. My toes curled when he raised a single eyebrow and grinned mischievously at me. "Nice pajamas."

"I don't have PJs." I blushed. "So I generally sleep in shorts and a T-shirt."

"I approve." He grinned. "Though I don't mind if you take the T-shirt off."

"You what?"

"I said, I don't mind if you want to get naked." He laughed and ran his hand down my back.

"Is that how you talk to all the girls, Zane Beaumont?" I shook his hand off of me. "It seems to me that you're a lot more uncouth than I thought."

"Why? Did you think I was a smooth operator?"

I stared at him for a second. "Well, I certainly didn't think you were a 'girl, let's get these clothes off of you' kind of guy. I assumed you had a little more finesse."

"I'm just a regular old Don Juan in your eyes, aren't I?"

"I wouldn't say that." I laughed. "You can't seem to keep them past a week."

"Why, you—" He burst out laughing and pulled me up towards him. "You're my regular little comedienne, aren't you, Lucky?"

I felt a warm shot of happiness inflame my body at his use of the word "my." It held a connation of closeness that I wanted to have with him. "Is that your way of letting me know you want me to tell you a joke?" I peeked up at his face and rolled my eyes. "You could just ask, you know."

"You know what I want to know?" He grinned at me and I leaned back into him, my back fitting into his arms comfortably.

"Why the sky is blue?"

"It's not blue right now. But perhaps you can tell me why it's black."

"Because there is no sun right now."

"Where is the sun?"

"Is this what you wanted to know? This is your last question. I will answer no more."

"Oh, Genie, how you tease me." He laughed and I grinned at him, trying to ignore the warmth emanating from his chest.

"One question."

"Or can I change that to one wish?"

"Hmm, I don't know …"

"What did you think of me when you met me in Lou's?" Zane's face was suddenly serious as he interrupted me. "I want to know how you knew you could trust me."

"How do you know I trust you?"

"You accepted this job. You're here with me now. You—"

"Okay, okay. I trust you." I laughed and paused, twisting to look at him. "I don't know why I trust you."

"Gee, thanks." He pouted.

"No, I don't mean it like that. I mean, I was your waitress, we were never really friends. And honestly, I never really had a great impression of you. We used to talk about you in the restaurant. Every Friday, we would roll our eyes when you walked in with a different girl. But inside, secretly, I was happy. I was happy to see you again, because you were always nice, always friendly, and always left big tips."

"And you thought I was hot, huh?" He wiggled his eyebrows and I punched him in the stomach. "Ow." He rubbed his stomach and groaned.

"Yes. I thought you were *cute*." I laughed. "Why? What did you think of me?"

"I thought you were the cutest thing." He laughed. "Every week, I told myself to take my date to a different restaurant, but every week I ended up at Lou's."

"Why?"

"Because I wanted to see your sweet smile, your non-judging eyes." He laughed.

I frowned. "What's so funny? "Maybe I wanted to see your sexy little walk as well."

"What sexy walk?"

"The one where you swing your hips."

"I do not swing my hips," I protested.

"Yes, you do. And then you stop at the table and ask what I want to drink and your eyes tease me with other possibilities."

"What other possibilities?"

"These." He turned towards me and I felt his lips come crushing down on mine.

I kissed him back and squirmed against him as I felt his hands on my butt, squeezing my ass cheeks. I found my hands working themselves up his T-shirt and my fingers traced the lines of his six-pack. Wow, what perfection. Zane pulled back from me slightly and pulled his T-shirt off and flung it across the room. His eyes bore into mine in silent challenge and I pulled my

T-shirt off as well and flung it across the room, allowing it to join his on the floor.

Zane's eyes left my face and fell to my scantily covered breasts. My half-cup pink lace bra was very sheer and I knew if he looked closely, he could see my nipples. I saw a vein in his neck throbbing and I was pretty sure he noticed. I ran my fingers back over his chest and across his nipples and then moved my hands up to his handsome face. I inched closer to him and brought his lips down to mine, kissing him with gusto and pushing my tongue into his mouth. All reason left my head as I tasted the minty sweetness of his toothpaste against my tongue. I took his tongue into my mouth and sucked on it slowly. He groaned before grabbing me and pulling me closer to him. I felt his hands on my back, undoing my bra, and as he unclasped it, I wondered for a moment what I was doing here. A very small part of me was screaming out that I was throwing out everything I had stood for in the last year. That I was wasting time with Zane because I already knew that he wasn't looking for anything serious. But the other side of me—the side that wanted to be right—told me to just go ahead with everything. This was the side that had been fantasizing about being with Zane for the last three months. This was the side that believed that he was a complex, strong, and passionate man, and that somewhere inside, there was a little boy just looking to be loved. The voice was telling me that just maybe, I could make Zane see that there was nothing wrong with love. That to have loved and lost was much better than to never have loved at all. It was a long shot, but I knew it was a chance I was willing to take. Zane Beaumont was in my blood. I knew that I couldn't go on without giving this relationship, or whatever it was, a chance—even if that meant throwing out the rules. Zane was a man for whom the rules were made to be broken.

"Is this okay?" he whispered as he pulled off my bra, and I nodded. A glint appeared in his eyes and he pushed me back on the bed. His mouth lowered to my breast and I felt his teeth on my nipple, sucking and nibbling hungrily. I groaned as he released a flood of desire in my body and my hands clung to his head, running through his hair and down to his back as he made me wet with desire for him. He switched his mouth to my other breast and licked around my nipple gently before biting down softly on it.

"Oww!" I yelped out at the pain of his bite.

"Shh." He put a finger to my lips and grinned up at me. He then kissed the valley between my breasts as his fingers played with my nipples and he kissed down my body, stopping at my belly button and sticking his tongue in for a few seconds. My body was on fire at his touch and I stilled as he continued his kissing down my stomach, and to my shorts. My legs widened involuntarily at his touch and I felt his mouth on my sweet spot over my shorts. Before I knew it, he had reached up and pulled my shorts and panties down and I was lying on the bed naked. I felt slightly self-conscious lying there in all my glory, but that feeling was gone in seconds as I felt his tongue in between my legs. Zane knew exactly what he was doing because I felt my whole body trembling as he worked magic with his tongue. He was quickly bringing me to a climax, and if I hadn't been   enjoying myself so much, I would have been slightly embarrassed at how quickly I was going to come. As soon as Zane stuck his tongue into me, I felt my body trembling and my wetness intensified. That didn't stop Zane though, it seemed to excite him even more. He lapped up my juices with his tongue as he slid it in and out of me, bringing me to another climax. My body shuddered and I moaned as I came again, and when my body stopped quaking, Zane kissed his way back up my body, grinning like the Cheshire cat.

"Who knew I was such a good lover?" He laughed as I looked up at him with lazy eyes.

"I haven't had sex in over a year," I muttered with a smile.

"But we haven't even had sex yet." He laughed and kissed me.

"Oh, yeah." I laughed and rolled him onto his back.

It was my turn now. I kissed down his chest, playing with his nipples and licking his abs. His stomach was rock hard, and I wondered how often he worked out. Zane's body stilled as I reached his shorts and put my hand inside to feel his manhood before I got him naked. I grinned at his moan as my fingers encircled his hard member, and I felt myself getting wet again, imagining him inside of me. He felt long and thick, and he was obviously as horny as I was. I ran my fingers up and down his girth, and he groaned as my finger movement was confined by his shorts.

"Lucky," he muttered at me through eyes filled with lust.

"Did you have another question, Zane?" I grinned at him as my hand stilled on him.

He pulled me back up the bed roughly before yanking his shorts off and throwing them across the room. He then pushed me down into the bed and rolled over on top of me, his eyes were glazed and I could feel his heart beating fast.

"You don't know how badly I want you," he groaned as he leaned down and kissed me. I felt his hand part my legs and he ran his fingers through my sweet spot, making sure I was still wet.

"Ooh," I moaned, unable to say anything else. I put my arms around him and wrapped my legs around him, bringing him closer to me. Our naked bodies were now crushed against each other and I could feel the tip of his cock rubbing against me. I opened my legs wider, urging him to enter me, but instead, he just continued to rub against me, his hands squeezing my breasts as we kissed. I groaned and wiggled underneath him, and he grabbed my arms and held me still.

"Hold on." I saw him reach over to his nightstand and grab a condom wrapper. I closed my eyes as he unwrapped it and put it on.

"Open your eyes." His voice commanded me and I looked up to see him staring down at me. "I want to see the expression in your beautiful brown eyes when I enter you and make you come."

I gazed up at him and felt him push his way inside of me. He moved slowly at first, and I felt the entire length of him squeeze into me, feelings of lust, pleasure, and delight enveloped me, and I cried out as he filled me up. He grinned as I yelped with pleasure and our eyes remained linked. He continued to hold me down but increased his pace, going faster and faster and deeper and deeper than I had ever known was possible before.

"Oh, Zane!" I screamed out as he took me to the brink of one of the most intense orgasms I had ever had in my life.

"Fuck, Lucky, I'm going to come," he grunted as he slammed into me. He released my arms, and I ran my nails up and down his back and shuddered as I climaxed. Zane collapsed on top of me and kissed my neck. I held him tightly against me and he rolled on to his side, with his arm draped over my waist.

"You're so beautiful, Lucky Starr Morgan." He traced his fingers from my waist back up to my breast and then to my chin.

"I can't believe you saw my driver's license," I groaned as he said my full name. "That's so embarrassing."

"You have to tell me why your parents named you Lucky." He smiled at me and leaned in to kiss my lips.

"I told you at the party, remember?" I laughed and then froze at my mistake. "Or maybe not."

"Argh, I'm guessing that was Braydon." He frowned and his eyes darkened.

"Yeah." I bit my lip, hoping I hadn't ruined the mood. "I hope that—"

Zane's lips crushed down on mine and I kissed him back, happily satiated. I giggled as I felt his hands reach in between my legs again. "Zane," I moaned as he played with me.

"Lucky." He laughed and licked my lips, bringing his hand back up and caressing my hair. "Ready for that movie?"

I nodded, eyes drooping as he pulled me towards him. He rolled over slightly and pushed the covers down and then pulled the sheets back up over us. "Come." He pulled me into the nook of his arm and I settled next to him, feeling warm and loved. "I thought we could watch a French comedy. It's an old favorite of mine."

"What's it called?" I yawned.

"No sleeping just yet, my dear." He grinned. "*Le Diner De Cons.*"

"Oh, I have no idea what that means."

"The dinner of fools."

"Oh?" I yawned again and snuggled into his chest. "It sounds interesting," I lied and he laughed.

"Trust me, it's hilarious. They did a remake of it called *Dinner For Schmucks* with Paul Rudd and Steve Carrell, but it sucked."

"Oh, I saw that movie," I groaned. "It was so bad."

"This one is a lot better."

"Hmmm, I believe you." I closed my eyes as he turned on his TV.

"You're not going to watch it, are you?" he whispered down at me as he rubbed my shoulders.

"I am too," I mumbled with a smile on my face.

"Uh huh." Zane's voice sounded amused.

"I'm watching," I mumbled, as I drifted asleep, listening to the French instrumental music that played along with the opening credits of the movie.

"Sweet dreams, Lucky," Zane whispered into my ear, and I fell asleep with a huge smile on my face. For the first time in a long while, I felt at peace and content. I knew that I was going to have a very happy sleep.

CHAPTER ELEVEN

"TODAY, I AM GOING TO SHOW you the Los Angeles that I love." Zane leaned over to kiss me as soon as my eyes opened. I stretched out and ran my fingers down his chest.

"So last night was real then?" I grinned, satiated and content.

"It can be real again in about a minute." He reached down and squeezed my nipple.

"As much as I'd like that, I would like to get out of the house today." I wrinkled my nose at him as he jumped off of the bed and pulled the covers off of me.

"Hey," I shrieked and rolled over.

"Let's have a shower." He reached down and picked me up.

"Together?"

"Of course, is there any other way?" he growled and carried me into the bathroom. "I'll wash you and you can wash me."

"I scrub hard, you know."

"You can scrub me as hard as you want." He pulled me towards him and kissed me softly. "Your lips taste like candy again."

"I'm sure they don't." I laughed.

"You smell like a dewy garden on a spring morning." He buried his head in my neck and breathed in. "You're intoxicating me with your smell."

"That's not all I can intoxicate you with." I pushed him back against the wall and grabbed his manhood. He was already aroused, and he grew even harder in my hands as I squeezed him.

"I thought you were holding back this morning?" His voice was husky and he pushed himself into my hand so I was rubbing his whole shaft.

"Well, I think I can spare fifteen minutes. It has been a while," I squealed as he picked me up and pushed me against the wall. I wrapped my legs around him and brought his head down to mine. I kissed him harder, and when I felt him enter me, I held onto him for dear life.

"Oh, Zane!" I screamed out as he slid in and out of me, every movement was tantalizing me and my orgasm was building up quickly.

"Oh, Lucky, you feel so tight and slick. You are always ready for me," he groaned and collapsed against me as we came together a few minutes later. I slid down from his waist and we stood there panting and holding each other.

"I need to start working out if we're going to keep this up," I exclaimed, trying to catch my breath.

"Maybe you should go morning, noon, and night," he whispered in my ear. "Because that is how much I want you."

"We can't have sex three times a day," I gasped. "We have work to do."

"We can squeeze it in." Zane turned on the shower and we stepped in, letting the hot water cascade down on us. I grabbed a bar of soap and ran it over his body, taking my time to feel and appreciate every inch of him. This man was perfect, from his muscular arms, to his toned stomach, and tight butt. I couldn't keep my eyes off of him, and I giggled.

"What's so funny?" He cocked his head to the side and licked his lips.

"I was just thinking to myself that last week I was wondering what you looked like naked, and now here we are."

"Do I fit the bill?"

"I don't think you could fit it any better." I laughed, caressing his ass.

"You have perfect breasts." He grinned and held them in his soapy hands. "They're the perfect size for me."

"Yeah, right." I shook my head. "They're too big."

"There is no such thing as breasts that are too big." He leaned forward and sucked on my left nipple. "I want to touch and play with them all day."

"Well, you can't do that," I moaned, as he licked and sucked. "Zane, please."

"Yes, Lucky?"

"I can't do it again," I groaned. "I'm too sore."

"Okay, we'll wait until tonight." He laughed and kissed back up to my face. "So what are we going to do today?" I asked curiously as we stepped out of the shower. Zane grabbed a thick cream towel and wrapped it around me and I smiled at him gratefully. It was nice having someone take care of me in this way.

"It's a surprise." He grinned.

"No fair."

"I want to show you the parts of Los Angeles that will make you go wow."

You make me go wow, I thought to myself. "Ooh, I'm excited."

"Good." He rubbed the towel up and down my body. "Spread your legs and stretch your arms out so I can make sure every drop is dry." I did as he commanded and stood there as he dried me off. This was the most intimate moment I had ever had in my life, and we stared at each other as he tenderly rubbed me down. His blue eyes were intense and focused, and my breath caught at the emotions I saw reflected in them.

"We're crazy, you know," I finally spoke. "Well, maybe just me."

"Why are you crazy, Lucky?"

"This moment is crazy. This wonderful, beautiful, special moment. I barely know you, yet, here I am, naked here in front of you and you're drying me and I'm loving it and I'm just so overwhelmed." I paused to take a breath. "You just used to be that cocky guy who sat in my booth, and now …" my voice trailed off.

"And now what?" Zane stopped what he was doing and stared at me.

"And now, you're the guy I'm having sex with."

"Am I just the guy you're having sex with?" He half-smiled and I was confused. Would I scare him away if I told him just how much he was starting to mean to me?

"No, you're the guy who makes me laugh and makes me tremble," I said seriously.

"Do you know that I've thought about this moment a million times?" Zane's voice caught and he smoothed the hair on the top of my head back. "Don't call me a horrible man, but every time I saw you at Lou's, I wondered what you would look like in my bed. I wondered if you tasted as sweet as you looked."

"And?" I grinned and rubbed his jawline.

"You're sweeter than I ever imagined. Thank you for taking this chance on me." His voice caught with emotion.

"Thank you for taking this chance on me." I ran my finger to his lips. "I'm so glad I came. Even though it's only the second day."

"I'm glad you're here. And you're right. We're crazy. But I'm glad we're crazy. If we weren't crazy, we wouldn't have moments like this."

"And God knows school isn't going anywhere." I laughed.

"Sometimes you just have to grab life by horns and ride it wherever it takes you. This is a good thing for us. School is important, and I would never say otherwise, but this is giving you real-world knowledge. You can go back to your history classes and tell everyone, 'Hey, guys, this is what really happened.'"

"Yeah, that will be awesome." I smiled quickly, trying to ignore the stinging feeling in my heart at his words. I didn't want to go back and tell anyone about anything. I was caught up in this moment, in the here and now, and I didn't want to be anywhere but here. I didn't want to be with anyone but him.

"That's my Lucky." He kissed my nose and grabbed another towel. "Now go and get dressed so we can leave."

"Yes, sir." I ran out of the room, giggling and singing to myself as I got ready.

***

"Okay, first stop." Zane parked the car and jumped out. "Welcome to the Los Angeles Plaza and the statue of Felipe de Neve. He's considered the first founder of Los Angeles."

"Wow." I looked at the statue in admiration. "I've never heard of him before."

"Most people haven't." Zane grabbed my hand. "Felipe was a Spanish governor, and his tenure was from 1975 to 1982."

"1975?" I grinned. "I didn't realize California was *so* new."

"I mean 1775 to 1782." He laughed. "Felipe was granted permission from Charles III of Spain to found and establish Los Angeles."

"I'm impressed you know that." I looked at him in admiration.

"Okay, I can't lie." He sighed and pulled me closer to him. "I looked it up. I never heard of Felipe until this morning when I looked up historical places to show you in L.A."

"You didn't have to do that." I was touched that he had done research for me.

"I wanted to take you to places that you love, and you love history." He shrugged. "It seemed like a sure bet."

"You're so much more amazing than I thought, do you know that?" I pulled him towards me and gave him a kiss.

"If it means I get lots of kisses, then I hope so." He kissed me back and then pulled me closer to the statue. "Let's see what the inscription says."

Felipe de Neve (1728–84). Governor of California 1775–82. In 1781, on orders from King Carlos III of Spain, Felipe de Neve selected a site near the River Porciuncula and laid out the town of El Pueblo de La Reina de Los Angeles, one of two pueblos he founded in Alta California.

I read the inscription aloud, impressed at how well he had remembered the basic facts. "It seems like you remembered it all correctly, smarty pants."

"Well, I'm not just all good looks."

"So where to next?"

"Are you hungry?"

"Yes." I laughed. "Are we going to get food? Please say yes."

"We're going to get a hot dog from Pinky's. I think it has to be the most famous hot dog stand in the world."

"I think I've seen them on the Food Network. Don't they have a long wait or something?"

"We won't have to wait. You forget my dad runs this town."

"Oh, well, sorry." I put on a posh accent.

"I'm joking." He grinned. "Well, somewhat. My dad is pretty influential, and we won't have to wait."

"Will I get to meet your dad?" I asked hesitatingly.

"I'm not sure." He frowned. "He's overseas right now."

"Oh." My heart panged for him slightly and I suddenly realized why he felt like such a kindred spirit. For all intents and purposes, we were one and the same. We were both alone in the world.

"But I can still introduce you to some movie stars, if that's what you're worried about."

"No." I laughed and grabbed his hand tightly. "I don't really care about actors and famous people."

"You're definitely one of a kind."

"I like to think so." I smiled up at him happily and we walked back to his car. "So now we go for hot dogs. Then what's next?"

"That'll be a surprise."

"You and your surprises." I shook my head and pretended to frown. I was delighted that he had gone out of his way to make this special for me. Maybe the Zane I was hoping to find was already coming to the surface. Maybe we would fall in love and this could be our happily ever after.

"Let's go get some dogs."

"Sounds good."

"So, Lucky, I want to know more about you. Tell me about what makes you tick."

"I love watching criminal TV shows. *Law and Order, Criminal Minds, CSI*, and *Dexter*—"

"I love *Dexter*. The books are great as well. Jeff Lindsay is such a great writer. His sense of humor is awesome."

"Oh, I've never read the books. I'll have to check them out."

"I have some at home. You can borrow them if you want."

"That would be great."

"Oh, by the way, the garage called me this morning, your car does have a head gasket problem."

"I told you." I hit him in the arm. "I'm not just some dumb girl, you know."

"Ow, that hurt." He grinned as he rubbed his arm. "I'm not sure I want to be your sub, I told you that already."

"You're an idiot." I hit him again.

"Lucky, I do own handcuffs, you know. You don't want to test me." He grabbed my hand and held it tightly. "I'd quite enjoy handcuffing you and—"

"Zane, I'm going to start to think you're only after me for my body." I was only half-joking, but I kept my tone light.

"Lucky, your body is just one of the reasons I like being with you." He let go of my hand and rubbed my leg. "You're the first girl I've ever been able to just be with, with no expectations. You're not expecting me to take you shopping on Rodeo Drive, you're not—"

"You mean I'm not going to be able to live my Julia Roberts' *Pretty Woman* moment today?" I pouted, and he laughed.

"We can go to the lingerie shop if you want. There's a La Perla in Beverly Hills that I can take you to."

"Ooh, you're going to buy me pearls. What's next, a diamond?" I joked but immediately wanted to slap myself for my gaffe.

"La Perla is a high-end lingerie store." Zane's voice was amused. "And no, no diamonds will be coming from me, I'm afraid."

"I've only been to Victoria's Secret before." I kept the conversation away from the jewelry talk and tried to ignore the hurt I felt, once again, at his words. *You know he's not looking for forever, Lucky. Just deal with it.*

"Then let's go get you a teddy. I'd quite like to see that."

"That's okay." I paused and bit my lip. I was starting to feel like all he wanted from me was sex. I hoped it was about more than that. I knew it was stupid to want more, but I couldn't stop myself from hoping and wishing. *Hopes are for fools, Lucky,* the little devil inside my head whispered. *Don't be a fool. Enjoy the sex, have some fun, hope for him to change, but don't get emotionally involved.*

I sighed and turned on the radio. I didn't want to keep thinking about and analyzing the situation anymore. Whatever was going to happen was going to happen. I just had to make sure to keep my heart protected. I had chosen to walk away from my rules. If I got hurt, it would be my fault. "Maybe we can go another day."

"After hot dogs, I'm going to take you to Griffith Observatory." He slapped his mouth. "Oh, shit, I let the cat out of the bag."

"What's that? A place we can see stars?"

"We'll be up in the hills and will be able to see most of L.A. from above. And it's an unusually clear day today, so we should have a great view."

"Sounds amazing." I sat back and listened to the sounds of smooth jazz coming through the stereo system. It wasn't the genre of music that I normally listened to, but it seemed to fit this moment.

"I'm glad you're here, Lucky," Zane interrupted my reverie. "In case you couldn't tell. I'm really glad you're here.

CHAPTER TWELVE

"I CAN'T BELIEVE WE'RE HAVING THE party tonight." I grinned at Zane as he prepared me a sandwich for lunch.

"I know," he groaned. "I should cancel it. I want to have you all to myself tonight."

"You've had me all to yourself for two whole weeks." I laughed happily. "I'm surprised you haven't gotten annoyed with me yet. We normally see each other for a few moments once a week, and now you see me 24/7."

"I couldn't think of a better person to work and sleep with."

"You don't let me sleep." I stretched and Zane stared at my breasts through my top. "Looking at something?" I grinned.

"Well, you can't not wear a bra and expect me not to notice." He stepped away from the counter and walked over to me. I hit his arm as he stood next to me and reached over to grab my breasts.

"Zane." I laughed. "I'm hungry and we still have an interview this afternoon before we have to get ready for the party."

"We still have time for a quickie."

"It's never quick with you." I jumped up and wrapped my arms around him and gave him a quick kiss. I ran my hands through his hair and pulled away as he ran his hands over my ass. "Okay, that's enough. I'm going to go change, and then hopefully, my lunch will be ready."

"You tease," he groaned and hit me on the ass as I ran out of the room giggling.

As I ran up the stairs to get some clothes from my room, I marveled at just how great the last two weeks had been. I had been slightly worried that Zane was going to have next-day regrets after we had sex the first time, but he had been great. He had been sweet and caring, and we had been inseparable since we arrived in Los Angeles. It was almost surreal—I hadn't expected us to get so close so quickly. It was even more wonderful than I could have imagined. I walked into my room and looked at the bed with a smile. I hadn't slept in it one night, and while it looked comfortable, I wasn't sad about that.

"Lunch is ready," Zane shouted up the stairs.

"I just got to my room, Zane," I shouted back as I went through my clothes. "I'm going to be a few minutes."

"Want me to come up and help?"

"No, thanks."

"I'm real good with getting clothes off."

"That's the least of my worries." I laughed and grabbed a pair of shorts, a bra, and a paisley shirt I had gotten at a vintage shop. I quickly got dressed and brushed my hair, letting it hang loose instead of in my usual ponytail. I applied some light makeup with a dash of lip-gloss, and smiled at my reflection. I looked pretty and in love, and I thought that this moment was perhaps the happiest I had ever been in my life.

"Aren't you ready yet?" I heard Zane at my doorway, and spun around.

"You are so impatient." I rolled my eyes.

"I missed you." He walked into the room and grabbed me, pulling me towards him. I clung to him and stared up at his handsome face. His blue eyes seemed so open, and there was a devilish spark in them.

"I am not having sex with you, Zane Beaumont."

"Who said I wanted sex?" He pouted and trailed his finger down my throat. "I just came to make sure you were okay."

"In case I fell in the toilet or something?"

"You know, you can't be too careful."

"Well, of course not."

"You are the girl whose car broke down in the middle of the night, after all."

"Indeed I am."

"And you're the girl who accepted a job with a strange guy and moved across the country."

"I know. What was I thinking?" I shook my head in despair. "I'm a silly, silly girl."

"Yes, you are." He kissed my nose. "So, of course you understand why I had to come up and make sure you were okay."

"Hmm, I still think you're not going to get laid right now."

"Well, then, let's go eat." He laughed, planted a firm kiss on my lips, and dragged me out of the room. "And by the way, your lip gloss tastes like a strawberry milkshake."

"Yummy." I stuck my tongue out at him and he squeezed my hand. As we walked into the kitchen, I picked up my phone to see if I had any messages.

"Everything okay?" Zane looked up at me, and noticed my frown.

"Yeah. It's just Leeza." I offered him a quick smile and looked back at the text from Braydon.

Hey Lucky, I miss you. I haven't heard from you in almost two weeks. Give me a call. I'm coming to Los Angeles soon. I'd love to take you around and show you a good time. I hope all your history knowledge is paying off and that Zane isn't being a complete and utter jackass. I saw Angelique last night, and she told me she dumped him. I'm sure he's pretty sore, so just ignore him. Text or call me.

I read the text message twice before putting my phone down. I felt my heart thudding as I accepted the sandwich from Zane. I studied his face to see if I could see any stress lines around his eyes. I was quiet as I ate my sandwich. Braydon's text had ruined my mood, and all of a sudden, I just wanted to be by myself.

"Hey, Lucky, what did Leeza have to say?" Zane looked at me from across the table with a guarded expression.

"She just wanted to know when I'd be back in Miami."

"Oh." He looked away. "What did you say?"

"I didn't respond. I don't really know."

"I guess when the documentary is finished." He stood up. "Are you done with your plate?"

I nodded and bit my lip as he carried our plates to the sink. "So do you have a date place in Los Angeles as well?"

"Sorry, what?" He turned around with a frown.

"Do you have a place you take your dates every Friday night here as well?"

"No." His reply was curt.

"Why were you in Miami?" I asked him cautiously. "Were you researching for the documentary?"

"No." He paused. "I had some other stuff going on."

"Like dating a different girl every week?"

"What can I say? I like the company of beautiful women." He walked away from me. "Are you ready?"

"Did you date Angelique?"

"Angelique?" He looked back at me brusquely. "Why?"

"I was just curious. You were very cozy with her at the party, but I never saw her with you at the diner."

"I never took her to the diner."

"So she was more than a one-time date?"

"Why are you asking me these questions, Lucky?" He sighed. "We have to get going, Mr. Johnson will be wondering where we are."

"Why is my bedroom so feminine?" The words shot out of my mouth before I could stop them. "Did Angelique design the room?"

"What's your sudden preoccupation with Angelique?" He sighed. "Can we talk about this later?"

"Why won't you tell me?" I continued, now frustrated. "Was she your girlfriend or not?"

"Look, Lucky, Angelique was not my girlfriend, and neither are you. Stop nagging me, please." He opened the door and waited for me to walk through.

Tears stung my eyes as I walked through the front door. My heart was beating so loudly that I was positive Zane could hear it. *You're not his girlfriend, Lucky. You're not his girlfriend.* That's all I could think about as I got into his car silently. His words hurt me to my very core and I stared out the window. *Well, that puts you in your place,* I thought to myself. We may be lovers and we may have a developing friendship, but that's all it was and all it would ever be. I sighed as I sat back. I wanted to go home. This was a lot harder than I thought it was going to be, and if I was honest with myself, I knew that I wasn't cut out for rejection. Not after everything. I wasn't the sort of girl who could and would put up with anything just to get the guy she loved. That realization hit me like a ton of bricks. I was falling in love with Zane, and I didn't want it to be an upward battle. I wanted him to know and realize, as surely as I did, that we had a connection. I wanted him to be the one pursuing me, and not vice versa.

"I didn't mean to be rude to you back there, Lucky," Zane started talking slowly as he drove. "You know I think you're special. I'm just not one of those guys that likes being questioned."

"I understand," I mumbled, continuing to stare out of the window.

"I met Angelique through my brother, Noah. We have a special relationship." His voice was soft.

"Does she know I'm staying with you?"

"I don't answer to anyone, Lucky. I thought you understood that."

"Do you love her?"

"I don't do love." He sighed. "If you don't think you can handle an unconventional relationship, we should end this now, Lucky."

"End what?" My voice rose. "You mean, we should stop fucking?"

"If you aren't able to separate sex from a commitment, then maybe we should." His voice was gruff. "I know you haven't been in a relationship in a while, and I understand if you can't do this."

"Do what?" I laughed lightly, trying to hide the pain from my voice.

"I know it's hard for girls to sleep with a guy and not develop feelings, but I thought after our conversation that you knew the deal."

"I do know the *deal*."

"I don't want to argue with you, Lucky. I've enjoyed two week so far, but I'm not going to put up with you trying to go down the relationship and jealousy road."

"What jealousy?" I said, feeling mortified. "I was just asking you a few questions. It's not a huge deal, Zane. What's your fucking problem?" I started shouting. "Why is everything a secret? Shit, we've all got issues. We've all been hurt. Deal with it. Okay? Just deal with it."

"Calm down." Zane's voice became cold. "Take a deep breath and calm down. We are going to pull up to Mr. Johnson's house in a few minutes. I don't want him seeing you look like a shrew."

"I don't look like a shrew!" I screamed at him angrily. I was upset that he had turned it all around on me and hadn't addressed my questions.

"Do you have the questions you're going to ask him ready?" He changed the subject. "We'll need accurate dates and names from him. Write down every detail. We should also confirm when he is available for us to come back with cameras."

"So we're not going to talk about it anymore?"

"Lucky, you have a decision to make." He looked at me briefly, and I quickly averted my eyes from his gaze.

"I have a decision?" I laughed sarcastically. "I don't think this is about me."

"If this is too hard for you, we don't have to continue." His voice was soft as he pulled up in the driveway. "I don't want to hurt you." I felt his arm on my shoulder and I continued staring out the window. I could feel tears welling up in my eyes and my head was starting to pound.

"Lucky, look at me please."

"What?" I turned to face him, and I was surprised by the pain in his expression.

"I don't want to hurt you." He sighed and rubbed his forehead. I was starting to realize that was his telltale sign for when he was feeling stressed out. "Maybe this wasn't a good idea."

"Maybe it wasn't," I replied slowly and sighed.

"I like you a lot, Lucky." His words were slow. "I love waking up to you in the morning. I love spending time with you. I love talking to you about history and movies."

But you're not in love with me. I stared at him and studied the cut of his jaw. It was so square and sharp. His face was so classically handsome. I thought he looked like he could have been a chiseled statue of a Roman god. He was so hard and unflinching. To some, he would also appear uncaring, but I knew that he was not at all what he appeared to be. Inside, he was one of the most caring and wonderful men I had ever met.

"Are you going to answer me, Lucky?"

"Let's go inside." I took off my seatbelt and opened the car door. I was not willing to have this conversation now. I needed time to think. I knew I should just tell him it was over, but there was a part of me that loathed the thought of saying the words. I didn't want to give him up already. He had wormed his way into my life, and I didn't want to let that feeling go.

"Okay, let's go and see Mr. Johnson." He nodded at me as he closed his car door and walked towards the front door. I followed him in silence, hoping that I wouldn't start crying during the interview.

***

"Thanks for allowing us the opportunity to do a pre-interview with you, Mr. Johnson." Zane shook the elderly man's hand, and I nodded my affirmation.

"No problem." The man ushered us in to his house. "We'll sit in the kitchen, if you don't mind. My wife has made some tea and cookies."

"That sounds great. Thank you," I beamed.

"No problem. We're happy to have visitors." He chuckled. "My Betty and I don't know many people here in California."

"You moved from Chicago, right?" I smiled, trying to impress him with my knowledge.

"Yes." He shivered. "We moved to get away from the cold."

"Sidney's arthritis couldn't take the winters anymore." An elderly lady came up to me and gave me a hug. "Hello, my dear. I'm Betty Johnson, Sidney's wife."

"Nice to meet you, Mrs. Johnson." I gave her a big, genuine smile, happy to forget about my conversation with Zane for a while.

"No problem. Sidney and I were happy to hear that a documentary was going to be made about residential segregation. You don't hear much about it these days."

"That's why it's so important for us to make this documentary," Zane interjected.

"Well, what do you want to know?" Sidney Johnson smiled.

"Everything." I laughed.

"Lucky's a history major, with a focus on the Civil Rights Movement," Zane explained. "She's also my assistant."

"Oh, so then you know some of what happened then?" Sidney looked at me with kind brown eyes. I grinned back at him and thought of my father. They had the same aura to them, and in some inexplicable way, I felt a certain connection to this elderly African-American man.

"I'd like to hear about it from your perspective." I looked at Zane and he nodded. "I had some questions, but I thought maybe you could just sort of run through your experience first?"

"Sure. Y'all better have a seat." He laughed. "And some tea and cookies."

"Sidney can talk, so I hope you have a long time." Betty laughed at us, and I smiled back at her.

"Thanks." I helped myself to a cookie and sat back.

"Well, I was born in North Carolina, you know. Back in those days, most of us were still in the South. I was born in the 1930s, right before WWII and the Great Depression."

"Sidney, that was long before WWII." Betty rolled her eyes.

"Well, WWII began in 1939. When were you born, Mr. Johnson?" I asked.

"He was born in 1930." Betty laughed.

"Wow. You look great for your age, Mr. Johnson." Zane complimented the older man.

"It's because my wife has treated me so well all these years." He laughed, and Betty hit him with a cloth.

"He is always trying to butter me up."

"So, like I said, I was born in North Carolina. But back in those days, we didn't really have any opportunity for jobs or school. My parents had six kids, you know. They had a lot of mouths to feed and they wanted us to get a good education."

"So they couldn't get jobs in North Carolina?" Zane interrupted.

"No, not back in those days," I interrupted. "The South was still very much full of Jim Crow. I'm sure his parents would only have gotten sharecropper jobs or work on some farm."

"Exactly." Sidney smiled at me and nodded. "My momma got a job cleaning houses for some of the rich white people in town, and my pops worked on a cotton field. They made okay money, but they got no school for the blacks in the town we lived in."

"Whites didn't want blacks to get education," I interrupted as I noticed Zane's puzzled face. "Back in those days, not many people went to school, only rich whites. Poor whites had some opportunity, but blacks only had access if another black decided to teach them, or if a teacher came down from the North."

"Thanks." Zane smiled at me, and I noticed the respect for my knowledge in his eyes.

"And, boy, let me tell you. There was no opportunity for any education in my town." Sidney shook his head. "So when the man came down from the North, telling my parents that he had jobs for them and that there was schools for us to go to, well, they got real excited."

"I was already in the North," Betty interrupted. "So my family didn't go through this."

"Yes, Betty's great-grandfather freed himself." Sidney nodded. "He was a butler for a rich white family in New York."

"They treated my family real nice." Betty nodded. "The whole family was real nice. They treated us well."

"He freed himself from being a slave?" Zane leaned forward eagerly. "I bet that's an exciting story."

"One we don't have time for today, Zane," I reminded him gently and Sidney laughed.

"You two remind me of me and my wife."

"Oh, we're not—" I started, but Zane frowned at me, shaking his head slightly.

"Continue with your story, Sidney," Zane spoke over me. "This is all new to me, and I'm excited to hear what happened next."

"Well, my pops packed us all up and we moved up to Chicago." He paused. "It wasn't normally like that, though. Most times, the man went up to the North by himself and got everything ready and sent for the family later. But my daddy didn't want to be without my momma."

"That's so sweet," I exclaimed emotionally.

"Yeah. Well, it may have been sweet, but I'm not sure it was smart." He shook his head. "By the time we got to Chicago, the Great Depression had hit. They weren't giving the jobs to blacks no more. There weren't enough jobs to go around, and we was at the bottom of the pile. It didn't help that neither of my parents had a high school diploma, either."

"So what did they do?" I leaned forward.

"They had some money saved, so they tried to rent an apartment in Hyde Park. It was a nice part of Chicago and they had good schools. They wasn't segregated at the time, so we could go to them."

"So it seems like all went well?" Zane looked at Sidney curiously.

"It wouldn't be worth a documentary if it went well, would it?" Sidney cackled and shook his head. "At first we thought it would. We got a two-bedroom place and my momma found a job as a cleaner for a nice family. But then they raised the rent. They wanted us to pay double what the whites were paying, or we had to leave."

"That's not fair," Zane interrupted again.

"There was no housing laws then." Sidney shook his head. "When we said we wouldn't pay more than the white folks, we got evicted. My parents, they tried to find another apartment in that part of town, but no one would show them any. Said we weren't qualified. Well, we knew that what they meant was that we weren't white."

"It happened all over Chicago, and New York, and Boston." I nodded. "Residential segregation was rampant after The Great Migration."

"The Great Migration?" Zane frowned.

"That's what they called the time period when a huge mass of blacks moved up North from the South. At first, the whites didn't mind, they didn't have the same institutionalized racism as they did in the South. I mean, there was still racism, but that was towards anyone new really: the Irish, the Italians—they were all met with skepticism. But the big cities, they grew too big too fast, and as jobs were lost, the new migrants were the ones that the hostilities were taken out on."

"They lost jobs due to the migration?"

"No, do you know about The Great Depression?"

"Not really?"

"Oh." I frowned, suddenly confused. Why was Zane making a documentary on a subject he knew so little about?

"You're very knowledgeable, Lucky." Sidney smiled. "Unfortunately, there was a lot of corruption in

Chicago and a lot of politics going on. They created a ghetto on the South side, and basically all the blacks were forced to live there."

"Forced?" Zane interjected. "How did they force you?"

"I'll explain it, Zane." I laid my hand on his arm and stared into his eyes. "Let's let Mr. Johnson finish his story."

"My pops eventually left the family." Sidney looked at us with intense eyes. "He thought he was a failure. Momma was still washing clothes. He never got a job. My brother got recruited by the mob and became a smalltime drug dealer, and me and my other brothers, we didn't really get no education."

"But you got a good job?" I interjected. "How did that happen?"

"They say everyone has a guardian angel, don't they?" He smiled suddenly. "One day I was walking down the street, getting up to no good, and I saw Betty running after a bus."

"I was helping my momma, she had sent me to go pick up some shoes," Betty interjected, rubbing Sidney's back.

"She looked so pretty and sweet, and she completely snubbed me." He laughed. "She was too good for the likes of me, and she knew it."

"I was from a good family. He was just a street boy." Betty smiled. "It wouldn't do good for me to associate with a street boy."

"I fell in love with her at first sight. I knew I had to do whatever I could to win her heart. I went to a school one of my neighbors had set up. He was self-educated and I was able to get a job as a delivery boy for a local store."

"He made it to college," Betty beamed proudly. "He only started getting a real education at fourteen, and he made it to college."

"Only because I knew you wouldn't marry an uneducated man." Sidney laughed.

"You mean date?" She shook her head, but her eyes were beaming.

"I mean marry, my love. I knew from the beginning that I wanted to marry you."

"So you changed your life around for love?" I felt tears well up in my eyes again. We had completely veered from the residential segregation conversation, but I was caught up in their obvious love for each other. "What a wonderful love story this is."

"Now you'll be telling me you want to focus the documentary on love and not the move." Sidney laughed and I saw him squeeze his wife's hand.

"I love a good love story." I smiled, and avoided Zane's stare. "Especially when it has a happy ending."

"Well, we have four kids and seven grandbabies, so I think it worked out pretty nicely." Sidney chuckled and stood up. "Excuse me, I have to stand up and stretch before my old bones get locked in one position."

"No worries." I stood up as well. "Do you want us to reconvene next week? We can pick up where we left off."

"You don't have to leave." Sidney stretched his arms, and I motioned to Zane.

"I think we have all we need right now." I paused. "Do you have a list of names and numbers for the other people you told us about from your neighborhood?"

"Yes, Betty wrote it down for you." Sidney nodded. "Some of them may be dead now, as we're getting on in age."

"We understand. And thank you, Mr. Johnson." Zane stood up and shook Mr. Johnson's hand.

"No problem, son. You be nice to this young lady here. She's a good catch." He winked at me. "And take it from someone that knows. Don't let her get away."

I blushed furiously at his words, and I could sense that Zane was staring at me. "Thanks for everything, Mr. Johnson." Zane's voice was light, but I knew he must be feeling annoyed.

"And, Miss Lucky, I look forward to seeing you again. Let me get a hug." Sidney gave me a huge hug, and whispered in my ear, "Your young man will come around. Don't give up on him."

"I … what?" I looked at him in shock, and he winked.

"Just let me know when you want to come by again. Betty and I will be here."

"Thank you, Mr. and Mrs. Johnson." I smiled at them as we exited the house. I got into Zane's car in a much happier mood than when I had gotten out.

"They were nice." Zane looked at me before he started the ignition. "And you were great."

"Thanks. They were amazing." I sighed. "What a perfect couple they are. And man, that story. How sad. But yet, so sweet."

"It'll make a good documentary."

I nodded and took a deep breath. "I wanted to ask you something."

"Go on." His voice was tense.

"Why are you making a documentary on the Civil Rights Movement when you obviously don't know anything about it?" I looked down at my lap.

"I guess I owe you an answer, don't I?" He sighed. I looked up at him, and he was staring at me with emotional eyes.

"If you don't mind."

"My brother studied history as well." He half smiled. "I still don't know much about it, though."

"Noah?"

"Yes." He nodded. "When we were younger, we watched a movie called *Imitation of Life*. I thought it was terribly depressing, but he loved it. He always wanted to make a movie about that time period. Like a look at race relations during the Civil Rights Era—he was almost obsessed with it."

"Oh?"

"I think we were so young when our mom left. And we had so many unresolved issues. Well, I think he wanted to displace his hurt. He wanted to understand the human psyche. Why people treated others the way that they did."

"I've always wondered that as well."

"Yes. I could see that." He sighed. "Noah would really like you."

"Will I get to meet him?" I asked softly.

Zane looked up at me with a pained glance. "No."

"Oh, okay." *Why?* I wanted to ask him, but I wanted him to talk about his brother when he was willing to talk about him.

"We should really pull out of their driveway." He laughed awkwardly.

"Yeah." I was disappointed. Just when we were beginning to get somewhere, he clams up again.

"Noah died last year." Zane's voice was low as he started the car, and I stilled at his words. "I found all these notes for this documentary in his stuff. I wanted to make it to honor him."

"I'm sorry." I wanted to reach out to him, but I didn't know how he would respond.

"He was my little brother." He clenched the wheel. "He was all that I had. And now he's gone. I'm making this for him."

"That's a nice way to honor your brother." My voice was soft and I reached over and squeezed his hand.

"He loved soccer. He was obsessed with it. When he was eighteen, I flew him to London and we watched a Chelsea and Tottenham match."

"Who?"

"They are two British football teams. He loved it." His voice cracked. "He said it was the best present I could have ever given him. Better than taking him to Amsterdam and getting him some weed and prostitutes." He laughed.

"Wow, he really loved soccer."

"He wasn't like me. He loved everything I didn't. He was a good kid. His biggest goal in life was to have a family. He was going to have all the kids, and I was going to be the uncle that spoiled them."

"The single uncle."

"Well, you know." He sighed. "Want to grab a bite before we go home?"

"We need to get your place ready for the party tonight."

"Dang. I forgot about the party."

"I can make you something to eat if you're hungry," I offered.

"That would be nice. Noah would have loved you."

"Sounds like he was a great guy."

"I'm sorry I made you upset, Lucky." He paused. "I didn't mean to make you think I don't love our time together, or that I don't want you, because that isn't true. I just don't want to end up hurting you. I can't do forever. And you're the sort of girl who needs a forever."

"You don't know that," I whispered.

"I don't know what? That you deserve a forever, or that I can't give it?" His voice was pained. "I know both of those things. But I'm selfish, and I want you. I don't want this to end just yet."

"Neither do I." I never want it to end. Never. I stifled a sigh and stared at his side profile. This man was reaching out to me finally—slowly, but surely— and I wanted to hold on to him and never let him go. But I knew there was an expiration date to our relationship. That one day—maybe in a month, maybe in a year, maybe tomorrow—would be the day it would be all over, and I would never be the same again.

"So you're willing to give me another chance?"

"I never stopped giving you a chance." I laughed.

"I don't deserve you."

"Have you ever been in love?" I asked quickly, anxiously hoping he would answer.

"I don't know if I should answer that." His voice trailed off. "Can I plead the Fifth?"

"I'm just curious." Please say no. Please say no.

"I was in love once, and she broke my heart." His voice was light. "And no, it wasn't worth it."

"Are you still in contact with her?" *Please say no. Please say no.*

"It's funny you ask that. I saw her recently."

"Oh." I looked out the window. So I guess it was true. Maybe Braydon had been telling the truth. Maybe Angelique was his ex and she had broken his heart. "So did Noah know Angelique?" I asked softly.

"I don't want to talk about it." His voice was strained. "I'm sorry, Lucky, but I just can't talk about it right now. Please don't take it personally."

"Okay." My voice cracked. I didn't know how to not take it personally. "Is there someone else you'd rather be with?" I couldn't stop myself. "I don't want to be a girl of convenience."

"Lucky, I can honestly tell you that right now, there is no one I'd rather have in my bed."

"Okay." I bit my lip and tried not to let him see how hurt I was by his words. I didn't want him to want me just in his bed; I wanted him to value me in his life.

CHAPTER THIRTEEN

"ZANE, DARLING, YOU LOOK SO HANDSOME tonight." A beautiful redhead kissed him on the lips as she entered the house. "And your place, just look at it. It's marvelous."

"Gina, so great to see you. You're looking as sexy as ever."

"Well, I do try, my dear." She twirled around and laughed. "And now a glass of champagne. Where is the champagne?"

"Follow me." He laughed, and I watched as he took her arm and led her to the kitchen. I felt the stirrings of jealousy erupt in me again and sighed as I leaned against the mantelpiece. I looked around the room and smiled at how cozy it looked filled with Zane's friends. They were all laughing and drinking, and they all looked glamorous and rich. To say I felt overwhelmed was an understatement—I recognized half of the room from TV and movies, and they all looked even more beautiful and handsome than I remembered from the screen.

"Oh, Zane!" Gina screamed and came running back into the room. "Such a naughty boy!" she exclaimed to everyone in the room. I saw a few of the girls rolling their eyes, and I smiled to myself. It seemed as if Gina was getting on everyone's nerves.

"So you're Lucia?" Gina walked up to me and looked me up and down. Her green eyes looked at me with disdain as she surveyed my khaki skirt and black top. I suppose she realized that my whole outfit cost less than her manicure.

"Lucky." I smiled.

"Lucia Lucky?" she sneered. "That's an odd name."

"No, my name's Lucky." I kept the smile plastered on my face.

"Oh, is it Irish?"

"Is what Irish?" I asked, confused.

"Your name? I thought Lucia was Italian, but if you say it's Irish, I suppose I'll have to believe you."

"My name is Lucky, not Lucia," I sighed and tried not to roll my eyes.

"You are an annoying girl, aren't you, Lucia?" Gina took a swig of champagne and sneered at me. "Though I suppose you have a good enough body under your ugly clothes."

"Excuse me?" I leaned forward, not sure I had heard her correctly.

"There you are, Lucky." Zane walked up to me and handed me a drink. "I've been looking for you."

"I was just getting to know your friend, Zane, she's *so* quaint." Gina grinned at him and linked her arm through his.

"Lucky is working on the documentary with me." He smiled at me warmly, and I felt a warm tingling in my belly as he stared at me. He was wearing a crisp blue and white shirt with a pair of black jeans, and all I could think about while staring at him was being able to rip his clothes off.

"Oh, are you a secretary?" Gina smiled at me, and I wanted to slap her.

"I'm actually a history major."

"Oh, you're still in school?" She laughed. "How cute, dear Zane, you went and got yourself an intern."

"Be nice, Gina." Zane shook his head and laughed, and I felt angry with him for not putting her in her place.

"Oh, Zane. I'm always nice." She pulled him towards her again and kissed him on the lips. "You remember, don't you?"

I stared at them aghast, and Zane looked at me and rolled his eyes. He detangled himself from her and whispered in my ear, "Are you having fun?"

"I will be later," I whispered back at him and winked.

He grinned and I felt his hand on my ass again. "Don't make me promises you can't keep, Ms. Morgan."

"Oh, I'll be keeping them." I grinned back at him, suddenly happy again. I was about to tell him exactly what I was going to do to him, but the doorbell rang.

"Oh, that must be Angelique and Braydon!" Gina cried out excitedly. "I hope you don't mind, but I knew you wouldn't. They just got into town today." She giggled.

Zane frowned. "Why would you invite Braydon and Angelique, Gina?"

"I know, I know." She rolled her eyes. "But you have to get over it sometime, Zane. Angelique was in love. She wasn't in love. It's a woman's prerogative. You can't hold it against her forever."

"You know I'm talking about Braydon."

"Oh, Zane. Get over it." She sighed. "Braydon is one of us."

"No. No, he's not." Zane walked to the front door, and I followed him with my heart in my mouth.

"Zane, darling." Angelique sailed through the door and gave him a hug. "It looks as good as I remember it." She smiled as she looked around the house.

"Thanks." Zane smiled and rubbed his head. "It's good to see you."

"And me, I hope?" Braydon stumbled through the door, slightly drunk, and looked around the room. "Lucky, there you are." He beamed as he saw me. "Lucky, I've been calling you."

"Hi, Braydon." I smiled at him weakly, aware that Zane was staring at me.

"Did you get my text?" He hugged me tightly. "I've been missing you."

"I got it." I nodded. "Sorry, I was busy."

"Well, I hope Hollywood hasn't been tempting you too much." He kissed my cheek, and I saw Zane coming towards us out of the corner of my eye.

"How dare you show up here, Braydon!" Zane's voice was angry.

"Gina told Angelique and me that it would be fine." Braydon smiled and stood next to me. "Plus, I wanted to see Lucky. I promised her a date when I got into town."

"That's Lucky's business, and you can figure out a time for a date outside of my house." Zane avoided eye contact with me and turned back around. "Would you like a drink, Angelique?"

"Actually, do you mind if I go upstairs and lie down?" she purred prettily. "My head is killing me."

"Sure." Zane looked concerned. "Do you need anything?"

"No, love." She smiled at him and rubbed his arm. "I know the way. I'll just head upstairs. Come find me in an hour if I'm not downstairs."

"Okay, take care." I watched Zane give her a quick hug and kiss on the cheek, and a knife twisted in my heart. The look Zane was giving her was as close to love as I had seen on his face.

"Thanks, my love." Angelique smiled and walked up the stairs. It was obvious she had been here before. I felt disappointment flood in me. I wasn't the first girl who had been here. I wasn't his first guest.

"So, Lucky, what are you doing tomorrow?" Braydon whispered in my ear, and I giggled slightly as his breath tickled me.

"Lucky, do you think you can come and help me in the kitchen, please?" Zane grabbed my arm and pulled me with him. "If you want to date Braydon, I can't stop you, but don't do it in front of my face," he hissed.

"What are you talking about?" I frowned, and yanked my arm away from him.

"I know you lied about Leeza texting you earlier." He pushed me against the counter in the kitchen. "If you're interested in Braydon, there is no need to lie."

"I never—"

"We're not exclusive. You can do what you need to do." He brought his face up against mine. "If you want to date a guy who brought another girl to a party."

"I—"

"He doesn't deserve Angelique." He laughed bitterly. "She is way too beautiful for him."

"Well, maybe."

"I don't know how she can date him." He shook his head. "I swear you women are really dumb sometimes."

"Why don't you go and talk to Angelique if it's bothering you so much?"

"I'm not going to go and bother Angelique." He shook his head and his voice softened. "She's not feeling well."

"Well, if she's not feeling well." *What about how I'm feeling right now? What about caring about me?* I wanted to shout at Zane. I wanted him to care about me as much as I did about him. I wanted our relationship to be about more than sex. I bit my lip as I felt his hands on me again.

"I want to pull your skirt up and fuck you right here," Zane growled in my ear and pulled me close to him. "You're so hot." He slid his hands up my legs and pulled my skirt up.

"Zane, no." I pulled away from him slightly. "There are people right around the corner."

"Wouldn't they be scandalized if they heard you screaming out my name?" His fingers slid inside my legs and up my inner thigh. "In fact, why don't we see?"

"Zane," I hissed as his fingers found my sweet spot.

"Are you wearing a thong for me, Lucky?" He grinned.

"No." I shook my head, blushing.

"Feel me." He brought my hand against him and pressed my palm into him hard. "We could be done in minutes."

"That's not a good thing." I laughed and he pushed me back against the counter.

"What's not?" He leaned down to kiss me, and I felt his hand creep up under my shirt and caress my breast.

"Zane." I put my arms around him and closed my eyes. Why couldn't we always have moments like this? Why did real life always have to get in the way and make things complicated?

"Lucky, are you in here?" I pushed Zane away from me as Braydon walked into the kitchen. My face was flushed, and I looked at him guiltily. I really needed to have an honest conversation with Braydon.

"Hey." I smiled at him, and grabbed a glass. "I was just getting a drink."

"Oh, I thought Zane was warning you away from me." Braydon laughed, and Zane glowered. "'Cos I'm a big, bad wolf and all."

"Braydon, I'll meet you in the garden in a minute, okay?" I pushed him towards the French doors. "Go out to the backyard. I'll be out in a moment."

"I'll be waiting, sugar lips." Braydon laughed and walked out.

"Hey," I turned around and faced Zane. "I can't wait for tonight." I sidled up next to him and he pushed me away.

"I don't want you talking to Braydon anymore, Lucky." He frowned, his eyes looking distant.

"You can't just ban me."

"Do not go outside and talk to him." His face looked stern. "I'm not going to tell you again."

"Why not?"

"He's bad news."

"Why is he bad news?" I shook my head, befuddled.

"Just listen to me." His voice was sharp. "I don't have to explain myself."

"Because it's always on your terms, right?" My voice caught. "I can't keep playing this game, Zane. You can't choose to tell me only what you want. It's not fair."

"I told you about my brother today, Lucky." His voice was pained. "That was a big move for me."

"And I'm glad you told me, but it didn't have to be a secret, Zane. I told you about my parents. You knew I would understand. I know how badly it hurts." My breath caught.

"You don't understand." He looked at me angrily. "We are not the same, Lucky."

"I'm not saying we're the same. I'm just saying I know what it feels like to lose someone you love."

"I don't know what you want from me, Lucky." Zane's eyes were bleak. "I don't know you well enough to share my deepest, darkest secrets with you. I'm sorry. That's not who I am."

"I didn't say I expected that." I bit my lip and sighed. "Look, you have guests out there, we don't have to talk about this now."

"Lucky, I'm waiting," Braydon called out to me from the doors and I walked out to him, averting my gaze from Zane as I left.

"I hope I didn't get you in trouble." Braydon frowned as I joined him. "Zane hates me."

"Why did you come if you knew he didn't like you?"

"I wanted to see you." He smiled impishly. "I missed you and I was worried about you."

"Why were you worried?"

"Zane's a little crazy." He shook his head. "I would feel horrible if something happened to you."

"Nothing's going to happen to me," I sighed. All of a sudden I was dreadfully tired. It had been another really long day and I was emotionally exhausted.

"Zane has anger issues." Braydon looked at me seriously. "Look, maybe I shouldn't tell you this, but Zane has it out for me."

"What?"

"I know, it sounds crazy, but he is really crazy. You know he dates every girl I'm interested in."

"Huh?"

"Zane has taken out all of my exes." He pulled out his phone. "That's one of the reasons I've been trying to contact you. I care about you. I don't want him using you."

"What are you talking about, Braydon?"

"Look." He opened up the photo gallery on his phone and started showing me photos. "You see all these girls? These are all girls I've dated at one time."

"And?" I was so annoyed that I didn't even look at the photos.

"Just take a look." He pushed the phone in my face and I looked down.

"Okay, and?" I was about to tell him to leave when I saw the next photo on the screen. "Wait, let me see that." I frowned and grabbed his phone. I scrolled through all the photos quickly, and I felt my heart freeze. I recognized at least ten of the women as Friday night dates of Zane's. "How do you know these girls?"

"They are all girls I dated." Braydon leaned towards me. "I don't want to make you jealous, Lucky. I'm not interested in them now. They were all good-time girls, I want a real commitment now, with someone like you."

"You dated all these girls?"

"Well, you know." He grinned. "Slept with, spent a few weeks with, that sort of thing." And then he frowned. "But then Zane always took them away from me."

"He stole your girlfriends?" I frowned. "Why would he do that?"

"He's crazy man." He shook his head. "And now he's after you. But you're special to me, Lucky. I can't let him get you, as well."

"I know some of those girls." I shook my head in disbelief. "I've seen him with some of them in the diner."

"I'm sorry, Lucky. I didn't mean to make your life a Hollywood movie."

"I need to go, Braydon." I stood up. "Thanks for telling me everything."

"Can I take you out to lunch tomorrow?"

"I don't know." I looked at his earnest face and felt something in me click. Wasn't Braydon the type of guy I had always told myself to date? "Maybe. Call me tomorrow, and I'll let you know."

"Awesome." He pulled me towards him and gave me a big hug. He smelled like sun, sand, and beer. But he was warm and soft, and I felt comforted by his embrace.

"I'll talk to you tomorrow." I gave him a kiss on the cheek and walked through the living room quickly. I needed to go to bed. I just wanted to be by myself. I didn't care if I was being rude by leaving the party early. These weren't my guests and none of them had been particularly nice to me. I certainly didn't owe them anything. They were Zane's guests and I didn't care if he thought I was a bad cohost.

I walked quickly through the room and ignored Gina's shrieks of, "Lucia, Lucia." She was lucky I didn't turn around and tell her shut up. I ran up the stairs and was about to sneak into my room when I saw that Zane's door was slightly ajar. I'm not sure if it was shock or curiosity that caused me to walk up to the door, but I crept to the door quietly and peeked inside. I saw Zane sitting on the bed, caressing Angelique's cheek. The beautiful blonde was lying in bed and saying something. I leaned in to get a better glance and I saw tears running down her face. My breath caught and I tried hard to hear what they were saying.

"I don't blame you, Angelique." Zane's voice was tender. He leaned towards her, but I couldn't see what he was doing. "My heart is broken, too." He sighed as he pulled back. "I don't know if I'll ever be the same."

"I'm sorry," Angelique whispered, and I wanted to burst into the room and scratch her. *You had your chance, bitch!* I wanted to scream. *Let him go. I won't break his heart.* My breath caught as a sob escaped me. I stepped back quickly and walked to my room. I closed the door and locked it, and then went into the bathroom. I ran the bath, stripped off my clothes, and turned off the lights before I stepped in. The tears started streaming down my face as soon I got into the tub. I submerged my face in the water and sobbed as I lay there. I sobbed with abandon and confusion.

Why had Zane been dating all of Braydon's exes? Had he been sleeping with me just because Braydon had shown an interest in me? It would make sense, after all. He had been coming to the diner for months and he had never been anything other than cordial and friendly to me as a server. He'd never shown any extra interest or asked me out. In fact, he hadn't shown me any interest until I had gone to the party and he had seen me with Braydon. Immediately after that, he had taken me to his house, taken care of my car, given me a job, and seduced me. He had changed my life and everything had gone so quickly. How had I gotten myself into this situation? This was why my Last Boyfriend Plan had been in place. It was to save me from unneeded heartache. It had been in place to protect me. But I had thrown it away in a heartbeat just to be with him.

I had, once again, allowed my emotions to supersede my brain. I knew that Zane Beaumont was bad news. I knew that a guy like him would only break my heart. And now, here I was, heartbroken.

I had a made a mess of everything. I scrubbed my skin as I lay in the bathtub. I couldn't believe I had withdrawn from my classes. What was I thinking? I closed my eyes and took some deep breaths. *It's going to be okay. You've gotten through worse.* I repeated over and over to myself. I should be happy for Zane. He had his true love back now. It seemed to me that he and Angelique were made for each other. I'd never seen him that tender and caring towards anyone before.

I yawned and closed my eyes as I leaned back in the tub. I felt so tired. I thought I heard a banging on the door, but I was too exhausted to get up and check.

All I could think of was Zane on a different date every week. And all of the girls were Braydon's exes. I had scoffed at them when I saw them. I had thought they were all so dumb. I had felt superior to them, knowing that he came in with a different girl every week, but the joke was on me. It was me who had believed I could change him. It was me who was sitting here with a broken heart. And all I had been was another notch on his bedpost—another girl he had taken away from Braydon. I sighed and turned over and realized I was still in the tub when I swallowed some water. I sat up quickly, spurting out water, and jumped out of the tub. I wrapped myself in a towel and walked into the bedroom, too tired to put on any pajamas. I jumped into bed and sunk into the sheets. I felt lonely without Zane there to snuggle with. I missed him. I started crying again. How could I miss him this badly already? I hated him. I wanted to scream and shout at him. How could he have done this to me? As I drifted back to sleep, I realized that I could stop Zane from thinking he had won. If I went back to Braydon and dated him, then it would show Zane that he hadn't stolen me from him. He wouldn't have won. *That's what I have to do,* I thought to myself as I fell into a deep sleep. *I have to date Braydon.*

CHAPTER FOURTEEN

"LUCKY, OPEN UP!" A VOICE WAS shouting through the door, and I groaned from under the covers.

"Stop banging!" I shouted back without opening my eyes.

"Open up the door," Zane's voice was furious and it sounded like he was going to break the door down.

"Okay, okay. Hold on," I groaned as I got out of bed. My head was aching and I was still wrapped in my towel. "Good morning to you, too," I greeted Zane as he rushed into the room.

"Where is he?" He ran to the bed, opened the closets, and then ran to the bathroom. "Where is he?"

"Who are you talking about?" I shook my head, puzzled.

"Braydon. You both left the party at the same time and you locked the door."

"I had a bath and went to bed." I rubbed my eyes and took in Zane's disheveled appearance. "Did you sleep in your clothes last night?"

"Did you sleep in a towel?" He grabbed my shoulders and looked down at my face. His eyes looked wild and crazy, and for a second I was worried that he was losing it. "Why are your eyes red?" He frowned.

"I don't know." I looked down.

"Wait a second." He rushed back into the bathroom. "The tub is still full. You didn't fall asleep in the tub, did you?"

"Kind of," I admitted sheepishly. "But I—"

"Lucky, do you know how dangerous that is?" His voice rose. "Why do you seem to have no concern for your life?"

"I woke up and went to bed."

"After you fell asleep in the tub. A tub that is full of water, I may add. Do you know how many people have died in bathtubs?"

"This isn't a horror movie, Zane," I joked, but he didn't crack a smile.

"You may not care about your wellbeing, but I do." He turned away from me. "I'm going out for a bit."

"I see."

"I have to take Angelique home, as Braydon just left her here."

"She stayed the night?" My voice cracked.

"Yes, of course." He sighed. "She slept in my bed."

"I see." I wanted to cry again, but I wasn't going to let myself break down in front of him. "I suppose you're back together now?"

"What are you talking about?" Zane's voice was loud and angry.

"Zane, dear, are you ready?" Angelique popped her head through the door. "I borrowed your shirt, I hope you don't mind."

"It looks better on you than me, so of course I don't mind." He smiled at her softly. "Go downstairs and I'll meet you in a few minutes."

"Okay." She left the room with her blonde hair swinging and I stood there in despair. This was truly turning into a nightmare.

"Are you going?" I wasn't going to give him the satisfaction of hearing pain in my voice. That was reserved for me alone.

"I thought we made headway last night, Lucky. I don't understand what's going on."

"Are you joking? You're the one that spent last night with Angelique," I hissed furiously.

"Angelique slept in my bed, and I slept in the spare room." Zane frowned. "How could you think I spent the night with her?"

"I don't know." I didn't want to tell him I had been snooping around the door the previous evening.

"Lucky, I like you." He sighed. "What more do I have to do to show you that?"

"I have one question for you." I took a big gulp and faced him. "Did you date Braydon's exes?" I watched as the annoyed expression left his face and a blank, tired expression replaced it. And that was when I knew. There was no other explanation. It wasn't just some big coincidence. "It's true, isn't it? You went out with Braydon's exes?"

"I asked you to trust me." He looked away and walked to the door.

"Just tell me the truth, did you date Braydon's exes?"

He stopped at the door and turned around and looked at me with a bleak expression. His stare was blank and he looked as cold as an ice statue. "Yes." The word was direct and firm, and just as quickly as it came, he was out the door and walking down the stairs. He had no explanation and no comforting words to give me. It was as if he didn't even care about how his words would affect me. But then, of course, he wouldn't care. Zane Beaumont was incapable of love. He had already told me he didn't want a relationship. I was the fool who thought I could change that. Who could make him see how great love was. When in all reality, I was only a fool, nothing else and nothing more.

***

Most women would have hopped on a plane and gone home if they had gone through what I had. But I decided to stay. I decided to stay for a two reasons: one being that I didn't have the money to go anywhere; the other was that I really liked Mr. Johnson, and I really wanted to make this documentary and do this research. Sidney Johnson was a part of history. He had gone through what I read about in my history books. There was no way I was going to give up this opportunity. Not for a coldhearted guy like Zane. I knew it would be hard—just thinking about him hurt—but I knew it would be just as bad if I weren't with him.

I took out my notepad and went downstairs to Zane's dining room. I sat at the table and made notes from our meeting yesterday. There was something about the Johnsons' love story that inspired me. I think it was because love changed his destiny. Betty's love made Sidney want to be a better person. When everyone else in his family had given up, when all the odds were down, he persevered and made it through. What had happened to his family was truly horrible. Residential segregation had been a bad thing—was still a bad thing—but he'd still made something of himself. The power of love was truly great. As I scribbled my notes on the page, I realized that I wanted this documentary to focus on the positives that had come out of Jim Crow and our horrific past. I wanted the documentary to celebrate those who had beat the system and toppled the odds. I wanted it to be uplifting. I wasn't sure how Zane would feel about the change, and I was scared. I knew he wanted to make it to celebrate his brother and his work, but I wasn't sure if he would be open to veering slightly off track. I was passionate about the changes I wanted to make, but I wasn't sure if I wanted to have that conversation with him.

I must have spent a few hours writing, because I didn't notice that Zane was still out until my stomach started grumbling. All of a sudden I felt cooped up and alone in the house. I didn't want to be here by myself. I didn't want to go through his fridge and make myself something to eat. It felt too intimate being in his house without him here. I closed my eyes and tried to forget everything I had learned within the last twenty-four hours. I didn't want to focus on the dull ache in my heart that made it hard for me to breathe and focus.

I picked up my phone quickly and dialed Braydon's number before I could change my mind.

"Hey, sweet pea."

"Hi." My voice was low and unsure. I didn't know what to say.

"Is everything okay?" His voice was concerned. "Sorry I left last night, I was kind of out of it."

"That's okay." I sighed. "Angelique was out of it as well. She stayed the night." *Why didn't you take her home with you?* I wanted to scream.

"She plays hard, she falls hard." His voice was light. "Want to go grab some lunch?"

"You read my mind." I laughed, as my stomach growled again.

"Need a ride or will you meet me there?" He was hesitant. "I don't want Zane coming after me with a shotgun."

"You can just pick me up. I'll be ready in half an hour."

"I'll see you then." Braydon hung up the phone, and I stared at it, wondering if I had made the right decision. There was something about Braydon that I couldn't quite figure out. He was always friendly and always seemed genuinely happy to see me, but there was something that was a little off about him and I couldn't quite put my finger on it. Normally, I would have avoided him, but after Zane had banned me from talking to him, along with the whole Zane-dating-all-of-his-exes thing, I had decided to continue to see him. It was like I was caught up in some sort of twisted hurricane and I couldn't get out.

***

"I hope you like tacos." Braydon grinned as we drove up to a taqueria. "They aren't expensive, but they sure taste good."

"I love tacos." I laughed, surprised at how at ease I felt with him.

"Shall we try one of each?" he asked, licking his lips. His hair had started to grow back and he looked surprisingly sexy.

"I don't know if I can eat that many tacos." I shook my head.

"I'll finish all the ones you can't eat." He grabbed my hand and led me to a table. "Sit here and I'll go order."

"Okay." I sat down and looked around me. There was nothing impressive about this hole-in-the wall Mexican restaurant, which was why I loved it. Braydon could have taken me anywhere to try and impress me. I had been expecting a swanky place in Beverly Hills or Hollywood, but he had taken me to a gritty part of Korea Town, and we were sitting at an old wooden table. I realized that I didn't really know Braydon. He was turning out to be a guy I would never have associated with being a big-time Hollywood star.

"Okay, here we go. We have *carnitas*, *lengua*, *carne asada*, shrimp, fish, and chicken." He carried the plates back to the table in a delicate balancing act.

"That's a lot of food, but they all look delicious." I reached out, grabbed a shrimp taco, and took a bite. "Oh, my, this is amazing." I laughed as sauce ran down my chin. "Oops." I grabbed a napkin and wiped it away.

Braydon laughed. "I'm glad you like them. This is my favorite place in L.A."

"Really?" I was even more surprised.

"Yeah, Noah and I used to come here every other day." He laughed. "Good times, man."

"So what happened to Noah?" I questioned, deliberately keeping my voice light. "I know he passed away, but what happened?"

Braydon froze as he was eating, and his brown eyes turned dark. "Zane told you he died?"

I nodded silently.

"Wow, I'm surprised. He never talks about Noah." He wiped his mouth, and took a sip of his *horchata.* "Noah was one of my best friends, you know. Zane always hated that. I think that's where the jealousy started."

"Because you two were friends?"

"Because I kind of took him away from Zane. Since their mom left them, it was kind of them against the world, but then Noah started branching out. He wanted a life outside of the Beaumont walls, you know? He was flashy and cool. But he also had a softer side. Zane is just intense and crazy all the time."

"Not all the time." I frowned. "He can be light and happy at times, too."

"Wow, you really drank the Kool-Aid, huh?" Braydon grabbed my hand. "I don't need to know what happened with you and Zane, I don't actually want to know. But trust me when I tell you, he is not a good guy. He's not like us, Lucky. He can't just enjoy life and be happy."

I sighed at his words. "I just don't understand. Did Noah commit suicide or something?"

"No." Braydon jumped up. "Hold on, I need to get some more napkins and water."

I watched as he walked away quickly and sighed when two teenage girls ran up to him, gushing and asking for his autograph. I didn't understand the secrecy behind Noah's death. Why did no one want to talk about it? I knew how hard it was to open up after a loved one had died. I didn't want to talk about my parents for months, but if someone asked me what happened, I wasn't hesitant or secretive. I saw Braydon signing one of the teenage girls' T-shirts and picked up my phone to check the time. I groaned when I saw five missed calls and three texts from Zane, demanding to know where I was and if I was okay. "I would hardly be able to text you back if I wasn't okay," I mumbled to myself. I pushed my phone back into my bag without answering any of his texts. I was twenty-two years old and Zane was not my keeper. Let him go jump off a cliff or something, I told myself. I couldn't keep up with him and his moods. And I didn't think I wanted to know if he had only used me to get back at Braydon.

"Sorry about that. Those girls asked for my autograph." Braydon stood at the table. "I'm really sorry about this, but do you mind if I take you home now? I have something I need to do."

"No problem." I jumped up. "I should be getting back. By the way, did you find out if Angelique got home okay?"

"Angelique?" Braydon looked at me in surprise. "She's a big girl. I'm sure she got home fine."

"She was really sick." I frowned. "You—"

"Shit, what did she say?" He leaned towards me angrily. "Did she say I gave her something? She's lying. I'm not—"

"Stop." I help up my hand in confusion. "I have no idea what you're talking about."

"Oh. Sorry. Forget what I said."

"What did she take yesterday?" My mind started churning. "Is that why she was sick? Was she on something?"

"How am I supposed to know?" he snapped and he drove off while I was still buckling my seatbelt.

"Did you guys take drugs before you came over?" My voice rose. "You were acting pretty weird last night as well."

"If you mean, did we smoke some pot, then yeah. Doesn't everyone?"

"I don't." I frowned and bit my lip. "You guys weren't high on weed. I'm in college, remember? I'm around potheads every day."

"Lucky. You're starting to annoy me." Braydon's sweet tone was gone. "I thought you were a cool girl and I came all the way from Miami to make sure you were okay."

"I never told you to come," I protested, now irritated.

"I'm looking for a wife; someone who is ready to commit. I thought when we first met that you were a possibility, but I don't think you are. Zane has poisoned you, obviously. I don't want to deal with this shit anymore."

"Whoa, what just happened here?" I looked at him like he was crazy. "I'm not trying to be a bitch, but I'm not even interested in you like that, Braydon. And that has nothing to do with Zane. You came on way too strong. You're a nice enough guy, but you will never have my heart."

"I don't want your heart." He laughed manically. "You're not cut out for our crowd, Lucky. Take my advice, leave Los Angeles and go back to Miami. Zane is going to chew you up and spit you out. And you're going to find your heart ripped out and dumped on the side of the road. And you know what? You're going to have no one to blame but yourself."

I bit my lip and looked out the window as he continued driving. I wasn't going to respond to his vile comments. Braydon's true personality was coming out and it wasn't pretty. I was so glad that I had chosen Zane over him—even if Zane couldn't commit and was just using me for some sort of sick revenge plot.

"Thanks for the ride." I jumped out of the car and slammed the door without looking back. I ran up to Zane's front door and paused as I realized I didn't have keys to get in. "Fuck," I muttered and wondered if I should ring the doorbell or call Zane. Before I could even make a decision, the door opened and Zane was standing in front of me with a furious look on his face.

"Where have you been?" His voice was deceptively low. "I have been calling you all day. I have been going out of my mind with worry."

"I went—"

"And was that Braydon? Didn't I tell you not to see him? Didn't I tell you to stay away from him?"

"He just—"

"He's bad news, Lucky!" he shouted, his nostrils were flaring and his face was red. "I don't know what else I have to say for you to get it through your skull. He's bad news. I don't want to have to worry about you as well. I'm already worried about Angelique."

"I'm sorry I'm not your precious Angelique," I blurted out, angry at his patronizing tone.

"Are you trying to make me angry, Lucky? Are you trying to make my blood pressure rise?" He sat on the couch and I sat down next to him, hoping he would calm down. "If anything had happened to you …"

"We just went to lunch, Zane," I sighed. "I get it, I really do. He's not a good guy. I saw it today."

"Oh, my God. What did he do?" Zane jumped up. "Did he give you anything?"

"No." I shook my head. "We just went to get tacos and then he had to leave."

"He most probably had a drop-off," Zane said cynically.

"What?"

"Nothing." He sighed and took a deep breath. "You can't just leave like that, Lucky, I was so worried."

"Worried about what? I'm a big girl. I can look after myself."

"I wasn't worried that you were hurt, Lucky." He turned towards me. "I was worried that you had left."

"I would still work on the documentary if I left."

"Fuck the documentary," Zane cursed, and paced up and down. "I was scared you left me. I was worried all night, and then this morning, I didn't know what to say or do. Then I had to take Angelique home, and she had to go get some prescriptions. And I hurried back to apologize for how I spoke to you yesterday and you were gone, and then my heart constricted. I was so worried. And you didn't answer your phone. Why didn't you answer your phone? I thought you went back to Miami. That maybe you were done with me. That I was too fucked up for you." He came and sat back on the couch and stared at me, the intensity in his eyes made them look like shining sapphires. "I don't want you to leave me, Lucky."

"You don't even know me, really." I heard myself speaking, but it didn't sound like me. "Why would you care if I left?"

"Why would I care?" He laughed bitterly. "Maybe because you're the first person I think about when I wake up in the morning. You're the reason I stayed in Miami for so long. I lived for those dates on Friday. I used to think it was because I was finally getting solid information, but it was because I got to see you. You don't realize it, but you're such a beautiful and bright human being. Seeing your face every Friday was the highlight of my week."

"I don't know what to say." My heart was soaring at his words, but I was scared to get my hopes up too high.

"When I was younger I used to read this poem by William Wordsworth, and—"

"Not 'I Wandered Lonely as a Cloud'?" I spoke up excitedly.

He nodded. "You know it?"

"I wandered lonely as a cloud, that floats on high o'er vales and hills," I began.

"When all at once I saw a crowd, a host of golden daffodils," he continued, and held my hand. "That's my favorite poem."

"It's mine as well," I said shyly.

"I'm used to it being me against the world. I always had to be strong. I had a brother I had to be strong for. I never wanted him to see me sad or depressed. But I was lonely."

"I'm sure Noah appreciated it."

"Noah wanted me to get out there." He sighed. "Ironically, he wanted me to be weak, and he wanted me to open my heart. Because that's what he did. He fell in love. Over and over again. And he got his heart broken and he would retreat into himself, but then he would get better. He always got better."

"A broken heart is a part of life, Zane," I sighed. "You shouldn't avoid relationships because you want to avoid pain."

"It killed him, you know." Zane's voice was pained.

"A broken heart killed your brother?" I frowned, very confused. "How?"

"He never got over it. I think this time he thought she was the one. He was so in love with her that when she dumped him, he needed something else. Something that I couldn't give him."

"I'm sorry."

"He thought he could fly."

"What?"

"The night he died, he thought he could fly."

"I don't understand."

"He turned to drugs." Zane sighed. "He was on angel dust, you may know it as PCP, and one night, he thought he saw Angelique waiting for him on a cloud, and he jumped off the roof of a building to join her because he thought he could fly."

"I'm so sorry, Zane." I squeezed his hand and tears welled in my eyes.

"It's not your fault." He sighed. "There are so many things I wish I could change. I wish I had been there for him more, I wish I hadn't been so closed off. I wish I would have killed Braydon the first time he tried to offer me drugs."

"Braydon?" My voice rose in surprise.

"That's why I didn't want you close to him. Braydon is a drug dealer." Zane sounded angry.

"But he's an actor."

"He doesn't make enough money to keep up his lifestyle, so he deals drugs as well." Zane frowned. "I've been trying to get enough dirt on him so he can get prosecuted as a drug trafficker. He's responsible for my brother's death."

"Angelique was your brother's girlfriend?" I hoped he wasn't mad that I had changed the subject away from Braydon, but as soon as he had mentioned her name, my heart had stopped.

"Yes. She still feels guilty. That's why I've been so concerned about her. I'm worried she's going to do something silly."

"I thought she was the girl you loved." I rushed my words, suddenly feeling light. "I thought she was the girl you loved who broke your heart."

"Angelique?" He laughed. "No, no, no. She was Noah's girlfriend for two years. She even helped me pick this place out when they were dating. She dumped him when her career started taking off. She got a big modeling contract in Italy."

"Oh, wow."

"She still loved him, but she didn't want to give up her career so she told him to move on. He couldn't take it. The pain was too much for him. He never understood why they couldn't be together when they were still in love."

"That must have been a hard decision for her to make."

"She regrets it every day of her life." Zane sighed. "But it's not her fault. It's Braydon's. Noah never did hard drugs. He only used to smoke some weed, but Braydon got him hooked. He was with Noah the night he died."

"He was?" I was shocked, but it seemed to make sense. "Why didn't he get arrested?"

"The police had nothing on him. He told them he had no idea Noah was on drugs. I knew, of course. I found out a few weeks before Noah died that he was on something, and I confronted him. We had a big fight, and he went and moved in with Braydon. I was going to go ask him to come back, but my pride got in the way and then it was too late."

"Oh, Zane, I'm so sorry." Tears streamed down my face, and I wiped them away quickly. "My heart aches for you."

"I don't want to make the same mistake twice. I don't want to keep my feelings to myself with you, Lucky." He took a deep breath. "Shit, this is hard. I really like you. Like, *really* like you. And I don't want to let that go. I think we could have something. I know this is coming from nowhere, and I know I can be crazy and moody and schizophrenic, but I want you to give me another chance. I want us to start again. I want to see if I can be the guy you've been waiting for. Will you let us start again?"

"Oh, Zane." I stared at his face and I wondered how I had never noticed the fear in his eyes before. I'd always thought he was so strong and hard, but he was a human being, just like me. He had fears and worries just like me.

"Answer me, Lucky." He grasped my hands tighter. "Please."

"When I lost my parents, I thought my world had caved in on me. And then a few weeks later, my boyfriend dumped me. And then I knew that was it. I knew the world was about to end. I couldn't breathe or even sleep. I never wanted to feel again. My life became perfunctory. I protected my heart. And I was happy with that. I wanted to make sure that the next guy I dated was the last guy I dated. I knew that I couldn't take one more heartbreak, and I didn't want to sleep around. But then you started coming into the diner, and all I could think about was what it would be like to date you, to make love to you, to be the girl with you on that date."

"About the dates, Lucky," Zane interjected.

"Wait. Let me finish." I smiled tenderly. "When I saw you at the party and we talked, all I wanted was to get to know you better. I wanted to talk to you all night long. And then I saw you with Angelique. I was jealous and I wanted to scream. I think that was when I kind of knew I liked you as more than the guy who came into the diner a lot."

"You did?" He smiled hopefully.

"And then my car broke down and you came swooping in like I was some damsel in distress, and you irritated the shit out of me. Yet I kind of liked that you were there to take care of me."

"I always want to take care of you, Lucky."

"I don't need anyone to take care of me." I shook my head. "I'm strong, Zane. That's what I want you to understand. I broke my rules to be with you, even though I knew it could all end with me having a broken heart. But I was okay with that because I know I'm strong enough to handle it. I would rather have a month, or a week, or even a day with you than no time at all. There is something about you that makes my heart soar. I'm addicted to you. Your smell drives me crazy and your kisses make me wild. And your smile makes me believe in angels. I don't need a promise of tomorrow when I'm with you, because today is all that matters."

"I want to be able to give you a promise of tomorrow, Lucky. I want to give you everything you deserve. You're stronger than me. You're more open than me." His voice cracked. "I don't want to promise anything I can't give you."

"I don't want you to promise me anything you can't give, Zane." There were tears in my eyes. "I just want you to give us a fair chance."

"Lucky, I haven't dated in years. I think that shows you I'm all about giving us a fair chance."

"You haven't dated in years?" I laughed and looked at him like he was crazy.

"Those girls I took to the diner, well, you were right. They were all Braydon's exes. I went out with all of them because I was trying to get information out of them. I wanted them to incriminate Braydon as a drug dealer so I could have enough proof to get him prosecuted."

"Oh."

"They weren't real dates, Lucky. They meant nothing to me. The only girl I could look at every time I went to Lou's was you."

"But who was the girl that broke your heart?" I asked with my heart in my mouth.

"The girl who broke my heart?" He frowned.

"The one you told me about the other day."

"Wait, oh, ha ha ha." He started laughing. "That was Lily Chen, she was my first grade girlfriend. I thought she was going to be my ninja warrior princess, but all she really cared about were Barbies and Legos. She dumped me when I refused to play Barbie goes shopping. She broke my heart for a week, and after that, I realized that love wasn't worth it."

"Oh, Zane." I laughed and shook my head.

"I'm fucked up, Lucky. I'm really fucked up. I don't know that I ever really got over my mother leaving us behind."

"Oh, Zane." I brought him in close to me. "No child can comprehend and get over their mother leaving. No adult either. You're not fucked up, my dear. You're hurt, broken, and rejected. But she didn't leave you, Zane. I swear to God she didn't leave you because you were unlovable. She didn't leave you because she didn't want you. I know there had to have been other reasons. There is no way that she left because of you."

"I don't understand why she didn't love me enough to stay. I don't understand why she didn't deal with my father for me and for Noah. Why didn't she love us enough to try and work out something? She just left us, Lucky. I can't get over that. I don't know why I was so unlovable. It was just me and Noah." Zane sobbed in my arms. "It was me and Noah, and I held it together for him. I wanted to be strong for him. It was him and me against the world and we could do anything. But then he went and got his heart broken and he couldn't cope. He couldn't cope and there was nothing I could do to fix him. There was nothing I could say to make it all right, and I lost him. I lost him just like that. It was him and me against the world, and he defected. He moved to Braydon's and I never saw him alive again."

"I'm so sorry, Zane." I kissed his forehead and kept him close to me. "But it's not your fault. You couldn't have known."

"Braydon told me that Noah thought he could fly. One second they were standing there drinking on a rooftop, and before he knew it, Noah was running and jumping off the roof, shouting out Angelique's name. Braydon didn't even have time to react. He was fucked up on some drugs as well, and by the time he realized what was happening, Noah had jumped off the building."

"I can't believe I ever thought Braydon was a nice guy." I sighed.

"He plays a good game. He's an actor, remember?"

"He lost it today, though. I bet he thought I already knew what he had done."

"What do you mean, he lost it?" Zane pulled away from me and pushed my shoulders back and looked into my face. "Did he hurt you, Lucky? God help me, but I will kill him if he hurt you in any way."

"No, no. He didn't do anything to me. I'm okay."

"Please tell me you won't see him again, Lucky," Zane pleaded with me.

"I won't see him again. Trust me. He's not the sort of guy I want to be friends with."

"So, are we good?" Zane stood up and pulled me up with him. "Are we going to give this thing a real try?"

"Are you going to go on any more fake dates?" I bit my lip. "I understand why you did, but I don't know if I could take it if you were still going out with other girls."

"I don't want to see anyone but you, Lucky."

"So we just continue as we were?" I held my breath, unsure as to what his reply would be.

"When we were on the plane, I told you that I never wanted to fall in love. I told you I could never be the one to give you that happily-ever-after. And I still don't know if I can be your everything. I don't know if I can be the man that you want me to be. But I sure want to try. Lucky Starr Morgan, I'm asking if I can be your last boyfriend?"

"You want to be my last boyfriend?" I gasped in shock. "Do you know what you're saying?"

"It's hard for me to say the words, Lucky, I'm not used to these feelings and I'm not used to wanting more from a relationship. But yes, I know what I'm saying. I want to be that person for you."

"You want to be my last boyfriend?" I laughed, deliriously happy. "I don't think I know what to say."

"Say yes." He laughed. "Say yes, and let me take you upstairs so I can rip off your clothes and do to you what I've been wanting to do for the last twenty-four hours."

"Zane!" I giggled. "You're too much."

"We have to remember a condom tonight, though." He wiggled his eyebrows. "I take it you're not on the pill, right?"

" No, I'm not on it."

"That's what I thought." He grabbed my hands. "You know there's a possibility that you're pregnant, right?"

"What?" I frowned. "How?"

"The bathroom."

"Oh." I flushed at the memory. Protection had been the last thing on my mind. "Oh, my. I didn't even think about it."

"I want you to know that I'm here for you, Lucky. Whatever happens. I want you to know that I'm in this with you all the way."

"Oh, Zane. I love you." I couldn't hold it in any more. "I really love you. I know it's not politically correct for me to say it before you, and I know we haven't known each other for that long, but I love you so much, Zane. I don't want to live without you. I don't want to be without you."

Zane's eyes glazed with unshed tears, and he brought me towards him and kissed me so tenderly that I thought that I was going to cry. "I love you, too, Lucky. I love you so much that words cannot adequately describe all the feelings in my heart. My heart is so full that it feels like it is about to break."

"Oh, Zane." My breath caught and I felt like my heart was going to burst with happiness. This moment didn't feel like it was real. I couldn't believe that I was hearing the words that I had waited my whole life for.

"Give me your hand, Lucky. I want you to feel my heart. This feeling, this heartbeat you feel beneath your fingers is because of you. It's for you. Everything that I am and everything that I want to be, from this moment on, is because of you." Zane's voice broke and he shook his head as if he was as amazed as I was to hear the words coming out of his mouth. "I don't care what happens any more. I'm not scared of what's going to happen. I don't fear us falling out of love. None of that is as important as what we feel in the here and now. And right now, I want you to know that you are everything to me. My heart is your heart to do with what you will. All I ask is that you hold it carefully."

"I will, my love, I will." I caressed his face. "I will hold your heart as delicately as I've held my own."

"This is it, isn't it, Lucky?" His voice was in awe. "We're the real deal."

"I think I've finally found my last boyfriend." I laughed and as we melted into each other with a kiss, I knew in my heart that he was my one and only. Without him, there would be no me. I wanted to stop time so we could be in this moment of love and wonder forever.

AUTHOR'S NOTE

Thank you for reading The Last Boyfriend. Zane and Lucky's story is continued in the sequel, The Last Husband. You can also read Zane's perspective of when he met Lucky in Before Lucky.

Please join my MAILING LIST to be notified as soon as new books are released and to receive teasers (http://jscooperauthor.com/mail-list/). I also love to interact with readers on my Facebook page, so please join me here: https://www.facebook.com/J.S.Cooperauthor. You can find links and information about all my books here: http://jscooperauthor.com/books/!

As always, I love to here from new and old fans, please feel free to email me at any time at jscooperauthor@gmail.com.

ABOUT THE AUTHOR

J. S. Cooper was born in London, England and moved to Florida her last year of high school. After completing law school at the University of Iowa (from the sunshine to cold) she moved to Los Angeles to work for a Literacy non profit as an Americorp Vista. She then moved to New York to study the History of Education at Columbia University and took a job at a workers rights non profit upon graduation.

She enjoys long walks on the beach (or short), hot musicians, dogs, reading (duh) and lots of drama filled TV Shows.

CPSIA information can be obtained
at www.ICGtesting.com
Printed in the USA
BVHW031942101021
618631BV00013BA/182